ATTACKED!

Jennifer had just taken a swallow of her punch when a burst of machine-gun fire erupted in the room, followed by screams and shouts of anger and alarm.

"Everyone stay where you are! If you move, you will be shot!" a loud voice called.

Six men rushed into the room, all six armed with AK-47's and wearing the traditional Arab headdress.

The two Secret Service agents guarding Mrs. Emerson stepped in front of her, both of them drawing their pistols as they did so. There were two shots, so close together that they sounded like one, and the two agents went down. On one side was a busboy, on the other a caterer. Both were holding smoking pistols, and it was obvious now that they had been planted in the crowd with the specific purpose of taking out the agents. Now, they joined the six armed men who had moved in to take over the room.

"Down, on the floor," the leader of the group said. "Anyone who stands up will be shot." He walked up to the front of the room, took the microphone, then turned to address the room.

"I am Aziz Hassan Faysal, warrior of Allah," he announced to the panic-stricken crowd. "Today the Islamic Jihad Muhahidin has struck a blow at the heart of infidel America."

BOOK YOUR PLACE ON OUR WEBSITE AND MAKE THE READING CONNECTION!

We've created a customized website just for our very special readers, where you can get the inside scoop on everything that's going on with Zebra, Pinnacle and Kensington books.

When you come online, you'll have the exciting opportunity to:

- View covers of upcoming books

- Read sample chapters

- Learn about our future publishing schedule (listed by publication month *and author*)

- Find out when your favorite authors will be visiting a city near you

- Search for and order backlist books from our online catalog

- Check out author bios and background information

- Send e-mail to your favorite authors

- Meet the Kensington staff online

- Join us in weekly chats with authors, readers and other guests

- Get writing guidelines

- AND MUCH MORE!

**Visit our website at
http://www.kensingtonbooks.com**

CODENAME: QUICKSTRIKE

William W. Johnstone

PINNACLE BOOKS
Kensington Publishing Corp.
http://www.kensingtonbooks.com

One

As the car turned west onto Decatur Street, John Barrone caught a glimpse of the sunset and saw that the sky was the color of liquid fire. To his left the Mississippi River made a large bow of molten silver on its circuitous journey to the Gulf of Mexico. In the heart of the city, steel and concrete towers loomed dark purple against the crimson sky, their windows reflecting a grid of melon-colored light.

The car window was down, and when they entered the Vieux Carré, going north on St. Peters, John could hear the sounds of New Orleans. Muted trumpets and wailing saxophones played by musicians with shining black skin and dark, soulful eyes spilled out onto the crowded sidewalks from the nightclubs. This was the haunting symphony of blues and jazz, the Crescent City's major contribution to American culture.

Through the open window of the car, John could also smell the distinctive night fragrances: the rich aromas of exquisite cooking, green bananas and pineapples just off the boats, as well as the delicate flower scents from the honeysuckle, jasmine, and wisteria that climbed along brick walls and over-hung the elaborate grillwork balconies of the Quarter's elegant old homes. A different perfume was given off by the French Quarter's painted ladies, who lounged in doorways or on street corners to practice their trade, marking the night with their own sweet, sensual musk.

The habitués of the narrow, winding streets of the French Quarter were, with the setting of the sun, just now beginning to awaken. By day they had slumbered as trucks plied the alleys and twisting thoroughfares, off-loading their cargoes of vegetables, meat, whiskey, and beer.

There were four men in the car: John Barrone and Bob Garrett were both members of a privately funded and very elite organization called the Code Name Team. The other two passengers were their prisoner, Mehmet Ibrahim, and Lucien Beajeaux, the driver of the car.

The Code Name Team to which John and Bob belonged was made up of ten people, seven men and three women. Their job was to "take care of things" that fell through the cracks. Terrorists, murderers, drug dealers, etc., who often got away with their misdeeds because of the technicalities and niceties of the law, were fair game for the men and women of the Code Name Team.

The team had no government connection; indeed, since they were extralegal, they were often at cross-purposes with the government. On the other hand, there were certain individuals within the government who knew what the team was actually doing, and from time to time those people would turn a blind eye to the Code Name Team's operations. On rare occasions they would even help.

In order to get things done, the Code Name Team needed some sort of operating cover. Thus, they often functioned under the auspices of a private detective agency, a personal security firm, or a bail-bonding operation . . . whatever was required to give them the operating authority they might need.

The team was sponsored by an international consortium of billionaires and multimillionaires. Though most were from America, other sponsors were from England, France, Germany, and Italy . . . with perhaps two or three from the Scandinavian countries.

As a result of the their "extralegal" status, everyone who joined the Code Name Team did so knowing that there was only one way out, and that was in a body bag. And because they had made a lifetime commitment, their loyalty, dedication, and support of each other bound them together as closely as if they were of the same blood.

Lucien Beajeaux was a private detective from New Orleans. He was not a member of the Code Name team, but Bob Garret, who was John Barrone's partner on this particular job, had vouched for him. Bob had worked with the former New Orleans policeman when Bob was still with the National Security Agency.

"How long it gonna take you to get to Chicago?" Beajeaux asked, speaking in a heavy Cajun accent.

"We'll get in at ten A.M. tomorrow," John said.

"Whooee! You be on the train all night? It more

better you fly," Beajeaux suggested. "You fly, you get there in a couple of hours. That what I'm goin' do when I go to Chicago one of these days."

"Ha!" Bob said. "Now, just what the hell would a Creole boy like you do in Chicago?"

"Hoo boy, ain't no tellin' what all I might do, I go there," Beajeaux joked. "Maybe I show those Chicago ladies somethin', I bet. 'Darlin',' I'll say, 'you ain' had no lovin' till you been loved by a Cay-john man from N'arleans.'"

"I'll bet those Chicago women are just waitin' on that," Bob offered dryly. John laughed.

When they reached the depot, the train they were to take was already standing in the station. It was a long, sleek, Amtrak train, painted in silver, red, white, and blue. As it sat at the station, the humming of electric motors was clearly audible, and wisps of vapor drifted away from the air-conditioning vents that were individual to each car. Some passengers were already inside, and they could be seen through the windows, reading, talking, or simply sitting there with their heads back against the seat headrests, waiting for departure.

"Park over there," John said, pointing to a parking spot near the station platform.

"Yes, sir, you the boss man," Beajeaux said, pulling into the parking spot John had indicated.

"I'm going to feel a lot better when we get Ibrahim on the train."

"You won't have no trouble," Beajeaux said. "The others think you fly to Houston."

"Yes, well, I hope the others took the bait when

we bought those airline tickets," Bob said. "Otherwise, we will have spent all that money for nothing."

"What are you worrying about the money for?" John asked. "It was Gil Bates's money. Bates has thirty billion dollars. He could've bought the entire airline and not felt it."

"Yeah, I guess so. Still, it seems a waste."

"It won't be a waste if we get Ibrahim out of here in one piece. We'll go by train to Chicago, then fly him to Houston. It is a circuitous route, I will admit, but it's the best way to go, because they won't be looking for anything like that."

"I am not a citizen of this country," Ibrahim said from the backseat. "You have no right to take me from here against my will."

"Hey, if it was up to me, I wouldn't take your ass anywhere," Bob said. "I would have dropped the hammer on you as soon as we found you."

"Drop the hammer?" Ibrahim asked, puzzled by the remark.

Bob held his hand in the shape of a gun, snapped the thumb forward as if shooting it, then shouted, "Bang."

Ibrahim jumped, and Bob laughed. "Scared you, huh?"

"I do not fear death," Ibrahim said. "I am a warrior for Allah."

"A warrior my ass. You put a bomb on the Dyna-Systems' Executive jet last year. Thirty-seven people were killed, including Mr. Bates's daughter."

"That happened in Sitarkistan," Ibrahim said. "The Sitarkistani court found me not guilty, I have been cleared of that."

"Yes, well, you haven't been cleared in Mr. Bates's personal court."

"You are being foolish. Private citizens in America, even those as wealthy as Gil Bates, do not have a personal court."

"Yes, well, you can tell that to the judge," John said. "Judge Gil Bates," he added, laughing.

"Anyway, you will not take me from here. My Islamic brothers will find me. They will kill you, and they will rescue me."

"They may find us," John said. "But I promise you, they will not rescue you."

"Think we ought to check things out before we take him to the train?" Bob asked.

"Probably wouldn't hurt," John replied.

"I know my rights," Ibrahim said. "I demand that you take me to the Sitarkistani Consulate."

"Funny thing, isn't it, John, how all the assholes who are trying to destroy the U.S. start quoting the rights they think they have?"

"Yeah," John said. He looked at Ibrahim. "In the first place, you towel-headed bastard, you've got no rights as far as I'm concerned. And in the second, even if you did have any rights, I would remind you that we are not with the police, FBI, CIA, or any other governmental agency. We are private citizens. That means we aren't bound by any of their restrictions."

"You . . . you aren't really going to take me to Houston, are you? You are going to kill me before we get there."

"Yeah, we might," Bob said.

"You cannot kill me!" Ibrahim said.

"Why should that bother you? Didn't you just tell us that you are a warrior for Allah, that you don't fear death?" Bob asked.

"Beajeaux, keep an eye on him while Bob and I check things out," John said.

Beajeaux pulled his pistol and pointed it at Ibrahim, then smiled. "I will do that," he said. "More better he try to run, I think."

John and Bob got out of the car and looked around carefully. When they were convinced the coast was clear, they turned back toward the car.

"Okay," John said. He opened the car and motioned for Ibrahim to get out. "Let's go."

Ibrahim got out of the car, his egress somewhat awkward because his hands were handcuffed behind him.

"Ibrahim, walk straight toward the train," John ordered quietly. "Don't look around, don't do anything to bring attention to yourself."

John, Bob, and Ibrahim started across the platform toward the train. Just to the left of the platform, on a track siding, stood a single boxcar. Suddenly the door of the boxcar slid open and four men jumped down onto the bricks. All four were wearing ski masks. Three were carrying AK-47's, one was carrying a shotgun.

"It is my brothers of the Islamic Jihad Muhahidin! Allah Akbar, I have been saved!" Ibrahim shouted.

"Bob, look out!" John warned.

The four armed men stood in a little semicircle and began firing, their guns blasting away as they swept the barrels back and forth.

Ibrahim started running toward them, a wide

smile on his face. Then the assailants did an amazing thing. They stopped firing toward John and Bob, and turned their weapons on Ibrahim.

"No!" Ibrahim shouted when he saw them aiming at him.

All four opened up at once, and Ibrahim went down with wounds in his chest, neck, and head.

There were several bystanders on the platform. Some were passengers getting ready to board the train, while others were there to see people off. When the first shot was fired, the civilians added their own screams and shouts to the bedlam as they started running in a mad dash to get out of the way. Some dived for the ground, others ran for cover. Beajeaux got out of the car and began firing across the top of it, at the four masked shooters.

The machine guns and shotgun chattered and roared. Bullets whistled all around John, Bob, and Beajeaux. John dived for the platform, then lay on his stomach on the bricks, his gun stretched out in front of him. From this prone position he pulled the trigger, and the gun bucked up in his hand, kicking out an empty shell casing as it did so. He was gratified to see his target grab his chest and fall.

Bob was hit in the thigh and the side, and he went down as well, but continued firing.

The firing continued unabated for about thirty seconds, though to John it seemed an eternity. A bullet cut through the sleeve of his jacket, but didn't actually hit him.

Suddenly a black Ford Bronco roared out onto

the station platform, and the two gunners who were still on their feet rushed toward it and jumped in. The driver whipped the vehicle around in a tight circle, the tires squealing in protest against the bricks. Once back on the road, the SUV began to roar away. John stood up to get a better shot at the speeding vehicle and, in anger and frustration, emptied his pistol at the back of the speeding Bronco, though he knew he probably wasn't hitting anyone from this distance.

John stood there for a moment, holding his pistol down by his leg, the breech open, indicating that it was empty. Scores of spent shell casings covered the brick platform, a visual indication of the number of shots exchanged during the shootout.

"Bob, are you all right?" John called.

"I was hit a couple of times," Bob answered, his voice slightly strained, "but I don't think it's anything serious."

"How about you, Beajeaux?" John called. "Are you all right?"

When there was no answer, John turned to look toward the New Orleans PI who had helped them.

"Oh, damn," he said when he saw Beajeaux. "Bob, we lost Beajeaux."

Beajeaux was lying across the hood of the car, his head resting in a pool of blood, his right arm dangling down, the gun hanging by its trigger guard from his index finger.

"Those sorry bastards," Bob said. "Beajeaux was a good man."

Looking back, John saw Ibrahim lying facedown and absolutely motionless, a pool of blood slowly widening beneath him on the brick platform. Two of the shooters were also down and motionless.

"If they were here to rescue Ibrahim, they did a piss-poor job of it," Bob said.

"I think they did just what they wanted to do," John said.

"What do you mean?"

"Ibrahim must have known some things they didn't want him talking about."

By now, cautiously, as if expecting another attack, the bystanders who had bolted to safety at the opening shots began to reappear. They were drawn by morbid curiosity to the little islands of death that were scattered about the station. Some stopped at the bodies of the two men John had killed. Others stood over Ibrahim, or went over to examine Beajeaux.

"Get away from him!" John shouted as he saw the morbid spectators begin to close in on the former New Orleans policeman. "Get the hell away!"

Frightened, the crowd backed away.

John went over to Bob, who was sitting on the ground, leaning against a light pole, bleeding from wounds in his side and his thigh. He was holding his hand over the bullet hole, trying to stem the blood flow in his thigh.

"Damn, why didn't you tell me you were hit that hard?" John asked in concern. He took off his belt and looped it around the leg above the wound. Tightening it, he made it into a tourniquet.

"How about the wound in your side?" John asked.

"It's not that bad," Bob answered. "I was pretty

much just nicked there. Not even bleeding that much."

One of the onlookers wandered over to John and Bob.

"Mister, what the hell was all this about?" he asked.

John didn't answer. Instead, he took out his cell phone and punched in 911. Even as he was dialing, though, he heard the sirens of approaching emergency vehicles, and as the first police car pulled up onto the platform, he closed the phone. Two policemen jumped out with pistols drawn.

"Get your hands up now!" the first policeman shouted.

John held up his hands. "You are a little late, Officers, the party is all over," he said. "What we need now is an ambulance."

"One is on the way," the other policeman said. Both policemen continued to point their pistols directly at John.

Four more police cars arrived, then an ambulance. The emergency medical technicians started looking over the bodies.

"Don't waste your time with them, they're all dead," John called to them. "This is the only man who needs your attention."

By now there were well over a dozen policemen on the scene and one of them, wearing captain's bars on his epaulets, approached John cautiously. Like the other policemen, the captain had his gun drawn.

"Who are you?" the police captain asked. "And what happened here?"

"We were taking a prisoner back to Texas," John said. "We were about to board the train when four men jumped down from that boxcar over there and attacked us. I think any of the witnesses here will verify that."

"That's right, Officer," one of the bystanders said. "The other fellas started shooting first."

"You were taking a prisoner to Texas on this train?" the policeman asked. "This train is going to Chicago."

"It's a long story," John said without going into an explanation.

"Where is your New Orleans Police escort?"

"We didn't have one."

"If you had extradition papers, you had to have a police escort."

"We don't have extradition papers."

"No extradition papers? Then would you mind telling me how in the hell you planned to get this man out of the state?"

"We don't need extradition papers; we are bail bondsmen," John said. He started to reach into his inside jacket pocket.

"Slowly," the police captain warned.

Moving slowly, John pulled out an envelope, then held it up. "Here is our license, and a letter, signed by a Texas judge, authorizing us to take Mehmet Ibrahim back to Texas."

"You're in Louisiana," the police captain said. "You need a Louisiana judge."

John shook his head. "No, we don't. There is a reciprocal agreement. Louisiana recognizes the rights of Texas bail bondsmen to return bond jumpers, just as Texas affords that same right to Louisiana bondsmen."

The EMTs picked up Bob and carried him back to the ambulance.

"I'd like to go with my friend," John said, pointing toward Bob.

"You're not going anywhere until we get this all cleared up," the captain replied.

"It *is* all cleared up," John said. "You've got my license, my letter of authorization—oh, and you'll also find a weapons permit in there—as well as my story of what happened. And as I said, any eyewitness here will back up my story."

"Cap'n, you know who this is?" one of the other policemen called from the car. "This here is Lucien Beajeaux. Remember him? He used to be on the force."

"Yes, of course I remember him," the police captain said. He looked at John. "Did you shoot him?"

"No, he was on our side," John said.

The ambulance pulled away, its warning signal making a honking sound.

"I'm going to take you down to the station," the police captain said. "If everything checks out, I'll let you go."

"All right," John said.

"Cuff him," the captain said to one of his officers.

Sighing, John put his hands behind his back as the officer applied the handcuffs.

Two

"How are Bahir and Jumah?" Aziz Hassan Faysal asked. Faysal was the leader of a cell of the terrorist group known as Islamic Jihad Muhahidin. Bahir and Jumah were the two shooters they had rescued from the train depot.

"Both have been badly wounded," Hakim said. "I think they need a doctor."

"No," Faysal said, shaking his head. "No doctor."

"But Faysal, without a doctor, I think both may die."

"Many of us will die in the execution of the fatwa," Faysal said. "If they die here or later, it makes no difference. It is the same with Ibrahim. He died by our hands, but Allah welcomed him as a martyr to the faith, just as if he had died by the hands of the infidels."

"I do not think Ibrahim would have talked," Hakim said. "Ibrahim was a man of faith and courage."

"Yes," Faysal agreed. "That is why his soul has forgiven us. He knows that Operation Islamic Justice is too critical to take a chance on it being compromised."

"Yes," Hakim said.

"When do we strike?" Dawud asked.

"Soon, my brothers," Faysal replied. "I have heard from Abdul Kadan Kadar. He will issue the fatwa soon."

Barksdale Air Force Base, Louisiana:

First Lieutenant Abdullah Afif Akil of the Sitarkistan Air Force ate alone at the Officers' Open Mess. In the parking lot outside the mess was a late-model Mustang convertible that he'd bought shortly after arriving in the United States. He would never have been able to buy the car on his salary as a Sitarkistan Air Force officer, but while in the U.S. on the guest officer exchange program, his income was supplemented by the U.S. Government so that he was drawing as much money as his American counterparts.

"Hey, Abdullah!" Paul Rigdon called to him. Paul was an Air National Guard Officer from Nebraska, and a student in the same class, transitioning into the A-10 fighter-bomber, officially called the Thunderbolt, but unofficially referred to by all who flew it as the Warthog. Paul was leaving the mess, but he came over to Abdullah's table.

"Hello, Lieutenant Rigdon," Abdullah replied.

"Listen, some of us are going to run over to Nacogdoches this afternoon to see the football game. You want to come along?" Paul asked.

"Football? Yes, I love football," Abdullah said. "I have watched the Sitarkistan national football team many times."

Paul laughed. "You're talking about soccer. We're talking football, real football, where a linebacker tries to tear off the quarterback's freaking head."

"Oh, yes," Abdullah said. "American football. I don't think I would like American football."

"You don't, huh? Well what about the cheerleaders?" Paul asked. "I know you will like the cheerleaders."

"Cheerleaders?"

"Yeah, you know, beautiful young girls, really short skirts, nice legs, great bodies."

"Yes, I might like that," Abdullah said.

"Uh-huh, I thought you might."

"The cheerleaders, what do they do?"

Paul laughed. "Well, they won't do a lap dance for you the way the girls do down at the Hot Box."

"Oh."

"Hey, Abdullah, you know what I can't understand? I can't understand why you guys keep your women all covered up from head to toe all the time. I mean, I know you like good-looking women—hell, you're a regular at the Hot Box. But you'll go home and marry some girl that the only thing you've ever seen of her is her eyes."

"It is important that our women be kept pure," Abdullah said. "They should not be defiled by the lustful stares of any man. Not even the man who is to be her husband."

"Yeah, but how do you know what you are getting? I mean, with your women all covered up like that, isn't marrying one of them sort of like buying a pig in a poke?"

"You are an infidel," Abdullah said. "I do not expect you to understand."

"You're right, I don't understand, but then I don't have to, do I? I say thank God for the good ole' U S of A and our half-naked girls. You know what I would do if I were you, Abdullah? I'd just stay in America. I mean, think about it, do you really want to trade that Mustang convertible you are driving right now for a camel? And let me ask you this. You have anything in Sitarkistan like the Hot Box?"

"No. We have no such place," Abdullah replied.

"I didn't think so. Anyway, we'll be leaving from the front of the BOQ in about half an hour. If you care to go with us, be there."

"Thank you," Abdullah said. "I will consider this."

Chuckling, Paul left the mess.

Abdullah left a few minutes later, thinking about his conversation with Paul. It was true what the American lieutenant had said. Abdullah was enjoying his stay in America. He liked the automobiles, he liked the liquor, and he especially liked the women. But the temptations in America were just too great. He realized that he could stay only at the risk of his immortal soul.

Abdul Kadan Kadar was right. America's decadence was a threat to young Muslims the world over. Young Muslims could not be exposed to the temptations of America without abandoning their own religion and culture. Something was going to have to be done soon, or succeeding generations of Muslims would be lost to the faith.

And that was exactly why Addullah Afif Akil was in America. What his classmate, Paul Rigdon, didn't know, what the U.S. Air Force didn't know, and what even the Sitarkistan Government didn't know, was that Abdullah Afif Akil was more than he seemed. He was a first lieutenant in the Sitarkistan Air Force, yes, but he was also a warrior in the Islamic Jihad Muhahidin. The IJM was a secret but growing organization dedicated to preserving the faith by eliminating the temptations of the decadent West. And before coming to America, Adbullah had sworn an oath to martyr himself to that cause.

When Adbullah returned to his room in the BOQ, he tapped into the Internet and opened his e-mail. The subject of the first e-mail to come up was "Islamic Justice."

That was the code he had been told to look for, and with a fluttering in his stomach and a weakness in his knees, he opened the letter. It was from Abdul Kadan Kadar.

I—with the help of Allah—call upon every warrior of Islamic Jihad Muhahidin who believes in Allah and wishes to be rewarded, to kill the Americans and plunder their money in whatever way they can. We also call on the Muslim ulema, leaders, youths, and soldiers, to launch the raid on the Great Satan which is the United States of America.

Allah has said, "O ye who believe, give your response to Allah and to his apostle, when he calleth you to that which will give you life. And know that Allah cometh between a man and his heart, and that it is he to whom ye shall all be gathered."

Almighty Allah also says, "O ye who believe, what is the matter with you, that when ye are asked to go forth in the cause of Allah, ye cling so heavily to the earth? Do ye prefer the life of this world to the hereafter? But little is the comfort of this life, as compared with the hereafter. Unless ye go forth, he will punish you with a grievous penalty, and put others in your place; but him ye would not harm in the least. For Allah hath power over all things."

Almighty Allah also says, "So lose no heart, nor fall into despair. For ye must gain mastery if ye are true in the faith."

Abdullah closed his laptop computer, then stood up and walked over to the window of his BOQ room. He saw some people playing basketball in the park on the other side of the parking lot. In the parking lot itself, a young, pretty female lieutenant, wearing shorts and a shirt that was knotted just below her breasts, was washing her car. As Abdullah looked at the cheeks of her butt straining against her tight shorts, he felt himself getting an erection.

"No!" he said, spinning away from the window. "I will not give in to the temptations of Satan's whores! I will answer the call!"

* * *

Addison, Texas:

When the Falcon Ten jet set down at the Addison airport, there was a chirp of rubber against macadam as the tires touched the runway. Don Yee, who was at the controls of the airplane, left the active runway, received taxi instructions, and started toward the executive terminal.

In the cabin of the aircraft there were four lounge chairs and one sofa that would seat three. Jennifer Barnes and Linda Marsh were sitting on the sofa; John Barrone was in a lounge chair right across from them.

"Don't look so glum," Jennifer teased John. "You look quite handsome in your tux."

"Bob is the lucky one," John said. "He's back at the headquarters recuperating while I'm here at this dog and pony show."

"Cheer up," Linda added. "Who knows, you might even enjoy yourself today."

"Oh, yeah," John said, dryly. "I can't think of anything I'd rather do than spend a Saturday afternoon at the dedication of some rich dude's skyscraper. I mean, if I weren't here, I'd be doing something like, oh, I don't know, watching a football game or something."

"Yes, well, it isn't just any rich dude; it's Gil Bates," Jennifer said. "He wanted to thank us for what you and Bob did in bringing the murderer of his daughter to justice."

"We didn't get him to justice, remember? We got his ass killed."

"For that son of a bitch, getting killed *was* justice," Jennifer said.

"Oh, wow," Linda said as the airplane taxied to a stop and the engines were killed. "Would you look at that stretch limo? I wonder who it is for."

A long white Lincoln limousine was parked at the ramp.

"It's for us," Don said, hearing her comment as he took off his headset. "I was just told the car had been given permission to come out to the airplane to pick us up."

"Well, now, doesn't this just make you feel like a movie star?" Linda asked.

"Next thing you know, people will be after our autographs," John said.

"Well, John, you just stew all you want," Jennifer said. "Linda and I are going to enjoy ourselves today. Right, Linda?"

"Right, Jennifer," Linda said, and as Don opened the door, the two girls, smiling broadly, hurried down the air-stairs and over to the car. The driver stood stiffly by the rear door, holding it open for them as they slipped into the plush, leathered interior.

Elgin Air Force Base, Florida:

Several airmen stopped to stare as Colonel Bob Jackson parked in the alert commander's slot in front of the pilots' ready room. They weren't staring at him as much as they were staring at his car. Colonel Jackson drove a mint-condition, classic 1939 Packard Darrin 120 Victoria Convertible. The sleek, low, racy lines of the car, along with the proud grille, had held up well over the years, and it was even more beautiful now than it was when it was new.

Colonel Jackson let them admire his car for a moment longer, then took a light, rubberized canvas cover from the trunk and fitted it over the car as part of a portable garage. He was just finishing when a Dodge Ram pickup truck pulled into the parking slot beside him. A captain got out and saluted.

"Colonel Jackson?" the captain asked.

"Yes."

"I'm Captain Hugh Taylor, sir. I'll be your wingman today."

"It'll be good to have you along, Captain Taylor," Colonel Jackson replied. "What do you say we go in and get our briefing?"

"Very good, sir."

Caruthersville, Missouri:

When the car stopped in front of the Delta Ag Air building at the Caruthersville airport, six men got out. Looking at the line of Gruman AG Cats parked on the flight line, one of them whistled.

"You are right, Tahir, there are so many airplanes here. I have never seen so many crop dusters in one place."

"This is an agricultural air center," Tahir replied. "Crop dusters from here are used as far north as St. Louis, and as far south as Vicksburg, Mississippi."

Akbar laughed. "From St. Louis to Vicksburg," he said. "And so they will be used today."

The six men went into the office. There, the dispatcher was sitting at a desk while two other men, identifiable as pilots by the flight suits they were wearing, sat on a leather sofa. One of the pilots was drinking coffee, the other was looking at a magazine. The man at the desk looked up.

"Yes, sir, what can I do for you gentlemen?" he asked.

The pilot who was drinking coffee stood up, quickly. "Marty, be careful with these guys," he said, suddenly growing suspicious at their unexpected appearance.

"Allah Akbar!" Akbar shouted, pulling a pistol. The other five who had come with him pulled their pistols as well. All six opened fire, and within a few seconds the two pilots and the dispatcher lay dead on the floor.

With them out of the way, Akbar looked at the others.

"All right," he said. "You know what must be done. Let us waste no more time."

Clarence Street, Dallas, Texas

The Voyager minivan pulled into a parking lot across the street from the DS Towers. Aziz Hassan Faysal, who had been driving the van, got out and looked up at the building, a towering structure of steel and glass. On the grass mall in front of the building was a free-form sculpture, and just beyond the sculpture stood a huge, black-marble slab with the word "DynaSystems" in white against the black.

Behind Faysal, the others began exiting the van, taking out several canvas bags as they did so.

Faysal looked at them, then held his arm up, his hand closed in a fist.

"Tonight in paradise," he said.

"Tonight in paradise," the others repeated.

Three

It was halftime in the game between the University of Tennessee and Auburn University, and because both schools had orange as one of their school colors, the stadium was ablaze with the pumpkin hue. The bands had just left the field, and with the score tied at 17–17, 92,315 fans were waiting for play to resume.

Although Auburn is known as the "Tigers," for some reason lost in the mists of legend and lore, their loyal supporters often refer to their team as the "War Eagles." Therefore, when a U.S. Air Force A-10 approached the field, an Auburn fan pointed to it and shouted the Auburn war cry.

"War Eagles!"

His cry was repeated by thousands of throats, and the crowd watched as the airplane banked, then made a low flyby over the stadium. The Auburn fans stood and cheered. The Tennessee fans, not willing to concede that the airplane was making a flyby in support of Auburn, stood and cheered as well. After all, this was a visual representation of the United States military, and the U.S. military was an all-volunteer force. The Tennessee team is known as the "Volunteers." Thus, the plane could just as easily be representing *them.*

The airplane pulled up at the end of its pass, then made a long, lazy 180-degree turn and started back. The cheering was loud and boisterous. In this time of war against terrorism, the fans of both Tennessee and Auburn were united by a spirit of patriotism, and they waved school pennants and national colors as the A-10 tilted down toward the stadium.

Suddenly a ring of fire appeared on the nose of the fighter-bomber. For just an instant the crowed thought it was some sort of salute. A portion of the crowd realized very soon, however, that it wasn't a salute, for explosive cannon shells and machine-gun bullets made of depleted uranium slammed into the stands at the Auburn end zone.

When the A-10 pulled up after its first pass, there were some in the crowd who were still cheering, not yet aware that the plane had just launched an attack against them. Turning sharply, the plane came back for a second pass, once again firing cannon and machine guns at the crowd. By now word was spreading quickly throughout the stadium that this was a deadly attack. The crowd panicked and tried to get out of the way. The machine-gun bullets and cannon shells caused terrible carnage, but the panicked crowd did even more. Hundreds of spectators were crushed in the mad rush as the crowd stampeded toward the exits.

* * *

Abdullah Afif Akil made several more passes, delivering his deadly cargo with grim efficiency. Finally, with the last round expended, he turned away from the stadium.

Though still alive, he felt as if he had already undergone the final transition. He was an angel of Allah, a soul without earthly desires.

Washington, D.C.:

Andy Garrison, the deputy director of Homeland Security, was watching the Illinois-Ohio State game when suddenly the picture on the screen switched to the game in Tennessee.

"Come on," Garrison grumbled. "What's the use of paying for the sports package if I can't watch the game I want?"

Suddenly, on the screen, he saw explosions ripple through the stands. Confused, he leaned forward. "What is this, a movie?" he asked. But even as he asked the question, he knew he wasn't watching a movie. There was something about the texture of the picture that told him what he was watching was real.

"We don't know any more about this than you do, ladies and gentlemen," the sportscaster was saying in a breathless voice. "You are seeing it happen, just as we are. What? What?" the sportscaster asked just off mike, though loudly enough for his question to be picked up. Then he cleared his throat. "All right, I'm being told now that we have a nationwide feed.

"Ladies and gentlemen, this is Charley Keith. Normally I would be bringing you the play-by-play commentary of the Tennessee-Auburn football game, but all that seems terribly insignificant now. To update those of you who are just tuning in, moments ago a United States Air Force plane began strafing Neyland Stadium. We don't know why, nor do we know yet how many casualties have been sustained, but we can report that there are many injured, and probably killed. Wait a minute, folks. We thought the plane had left, but here it comes again!"

Andy Garrison called his liaison in the FBI. "Peter, turn on the TV," he said.

"I'm watching it," Peter Simmons said.

"Has POTUS been informed?"

"The President of the United States has been informed," Peter answered.

"Are we doing anything?"

"The Air Force is scrambling fighter jets," Peter replied. "Though that's a little like shutting the barn door after the horse is gone."

"Yes, well, we can't undo what has been done. But maybe we can shoot this bastard down, whoever the hell he is," Andy said.

"Wait, are you watching this? He's coming back," Peter said in alarm.

On screen, the A-10 was heading straight for the camera.

"He doesn't seem to be shooting this time," Charley Keith, the sportscaster was saying. "Hopefully, he's run out of ammunition."

"Charley, he's coming straight for us," the color commentator said.

"Bobby's right, folks," Charley said. "He's coming right at us. We should be able to get a really good look this time."

"My God, Charley! He's not turning away!" Bobby shouted.

On screen the airplane got bigger and bigger until it filled the screen. Then there was nothing but a few lines across the screen, followed by snow, then blackness. Almost instantly thereafter, the picture returned to the studio where, normally, a sports news reporter would be updating the nation on the latest scores of all major college games in progress. But now the reporter was sitting behind the familiar curved desk in front of a large board filled with team names and scores, holding his finger to his earpiece. He nodded, then looked at the camera. As the camera moved in, the patina of sweat that covered his face was clearly visible. He licked his lips.

"Uh, ladies and gentlemen, there has obviously been some sort of major malfunction in our feed from Knoxville. We'll get that taken care of as quickly as we can. In the meantime, we're—" He halted in mid-sentence, obviously listening to instructions in his earphone, then nodded. "Yes, we're going to our News Central desk."

Elgin AFB, Florida:

The F-15's Colonel Bob Jackson and Captain Hugh Taylor were flying roared into the sky on pillars of fire. Colonel Jackson felt his weight increase many times from the effects of acceleration. Working hard to overcome the G forces, he lifted his hand to the radio-control panel and changed frequencies from tower to command.

"Charley-Charley, this is Gunslinger One with flight of two, requesting a vector and clearance."

"Gunslinger One, take a heading of two-six-zero. You are cleared at any altitude, proceed at maximum possible speed. Squawk your parrot and scramble, please, sir."

"Roger, squawking," Colonel Jackson replied. He "squawked his parrot" by pushing a button on his IFF that would emit a coded signal, thus identifying him as friendly. He also turned a switch on his radio that would make it impossible for anyone listening in to understand what was being said. "Scrambled," he reported.

The voice of Charley-Charley came over the headset once more.

"Gunslinger One, my authenticator is Mad Dog. I say again, my authenticator is Mad Dog. Respond, please."

"Seabiscuit," Colonel Jackson replied, responding with the correct code to authorize the reception of top-secret information.

"You are cleared to engage."

"Roger," Jackson replied.

"Colonel, I can see smoke ahead," Captain Taylor said.

"Light up the afterburner, Captain," Jackson replied. "If that sonofabitch is anywhere in the area, I don't intend to let him to get away."

"Roger, lighting the burner."

The afterburners of both F-15's kicked in with a boom, increasing the speed so dramatically that, once again, the pilots could feel themselves being pressed back into their seats. A three-minute burn took them to the site of the billowing smoke, then both aircraft throttled down as they orbited the stadium to check out the scene.

"Charley-Charley, this is Gunslinger One. We're on station," Colonel Jackson called.

"Your target is an A-10," Sector Control replied.

"Negative, there is no target," Jackson said as he banked sharply around the burning press box.

"Has the target departed the area?"

"I think he crashed into the press box."

"Please confirm."

"Roger."

Colonel Jackson and Captain Taylor made a very low flyby to examine the press box. A large percentage of the crowd was still in the stands, and not understanding that the two fighters had been sent to help them, they dived under the seats to avoid an attack.

"Did you see anything definite, Captain?" Colonel Jackson asked as they pulled up from their first pass.

"Negative."

"Give me a covering orbit. I'm going back for another look," Colonel Jackson said.

"I have you covered, sir."

Captain Taylor flew a wide orbit high above the stadium, while Colonel Jackson dropped gear and flaps and made another low pass, this time coming down even below the top level of the bleachers.

There were some in the crowd who thought he was actually going to land on the football field, but in truth, he had just made his airplane "dirty" so he could perform the very low, and very slow, flyby.

Although the activities of the two F-15's were cause for concern and curiosity in the stands, there was no reaction at all from the press box. That was because Charley Keith, Bobby Sawyer, and every other occupant of the press box lay dead in the twisted and burning wreckage.

Memphis, Tennessee:

The University of Tennessee had many fans in Memphis; therefore much of the city was aware of what was happening on the other side of the state. Sitting in front of their TV sets, they watched in horror as the airplane, apparently an Air Force fighter, shot up the stadium, then crashed into the press box. Now, talking among themselves, many decided that the insane act was that of an Air Force pilot gone berserk.

"It's like a disgruntled postman shooting up the post office, or kids shooting up a school," many told each other.

Even as the residents of Memphis contemplated the terrible event, two Gruman AG Cats, crop-dusting airplanes, were approaching the city from the north. Because crop dusting is a common event in the Arkansas, Tennessee, and Mississippi farmland surrounding the city, such planes were familiar sights, so no one paid any attention to them, including the motorists who were, at that moment, crossing the river on Memphis's two bridges.

The two airplanes had been flying in a loose formation, but they separated as they approached the city. One of the planes headed toward the Frisco Bridge, while the other headed toward the Hernando DeSoto Bridge. The large-capacity hoppers of the two planes, normally filled with agricultural spray, were now filled with gasoline.

A fuel tanker truck was crossing the DeSoto Bridge, and the pilot of the approaching crop duster managed to crash right into the truck. And although both planes detonated with huge fireballs, the explosion on the DeSoto Bridge was much more spectacular. It was short-lived, however, because its very intensity dropped the bridge into the Mississippi River, quickly extinguishing the flames.

Twelve cars and a bus were involved in the attack on the Frisco Bridge. A huge column of smoke roiled up from the fiercely burning vehicles, climbing high into the blue, cloudless sky over the bridge.

At the same time as the attack in Memphis, other crop-dusting planes were attacking bridges in Vicksburg, Mississippi, as well as Caruthersville, Cape Girardeau, and St. Louis, Missouri. Within a period of ten minutes, the Mississippi River became a barrier that halted nearly all ground transportation between the eastern and western halves of the United States.

* * *

Dallas, Texas:

In Dallas, nearly a hundred people, as yet unaware of the attacks going on in the rest of the country, were gathered at an upscale reception. The party was being given by Gilbert Bates, the multibillionaire head of a computer software company called Dyna-Systems. Bates was celebrating the opening of his world headquarters, known as DS Towers, a sixty-seven-story skyscraper in downtown Dallas.

The guest list of the reception read like the roster of America's power elite: politicians, media moguls, financiers, movie and television personalities, sports figures, and other technology czars. Also in attendance was Karen Emerson, the wife of President Bill Emerson of the United States.

This was also the affair that John Barrone, Jennifer Barnes, Don Yee, and Linda Marsh were attending. It was a strictly dress-up social event, with a catered reception and chamber orchestra.

The reception was being held in a large room on the sixty-sixth floor of the DS Towers. John, who was standing with Jennifer in one corner of the room, stuck his finger down in his collar and pulled it away from his neck. Jennifer laughed.

"What are you laughing at?" he asked.

"You," Jennifer said.

"Why?"

Jennifer pantomimed his pulling the collar away. "Why don't you just hang a sign around your neck that says: 'I really, really don't want to be here.'"

"What are you talking about? John loves it here," Don said.

"Yeah. Where else would I be able to indulge myself in those little cream-cheese and watercress sandwiches, that mountain of broccoli and cauliflower, and whatever the hell that mucus-looking gunk is that you're supposed to dip them in?"

"You're incorrigible," Jennifer said.

"Actually, I could handle it a little better if I didn't have to put up with the elevator music. Live elevator music, no less," John said.

"Elevator music? That happens to be one of the foremost chamber orchestras in the country," Linda Marsh said. "And I don't think Vivaldi would appreciate having his music referred to as elevator music."

"Yeah, well, you'd think a man with all Bates's money could afford to get someone like Garth Brooks, or Randy Travis."

"Leave it to John to want shit-kicking music at a party like this," Don said, laughing.

"Hey, any song that celebrates bad women and good booze can't be all bad," John said.

Suddenly the orchestra played a fanfare, and Gil Bates walked to the front of the room.

"Ladies and gentlemen, may I have your attention please?" He said.

The room grew quiet.

"I want to thank all of you for coming to this, the grand opening of DS Towers. DynaSystems is . . ."

"This is where I go to the men's room," John whispered to the others.

"Do you really have to go? Or is this just an excuse to get away from the speech?" Jennifer asked.

John smiled. "Either way, it's the same," he said.

John really did have to go to the rest room, but decided it would be better to call as little attention to himself as possible. Therefore, rather than leaving by the main entrance, he slipped out through a service door over in one corner of the room. Not only was this exit out of the way, it was also hidden by a large potted palm.

There were two rest-room complexes out in the hall, one right across the hall from the main door leading into the ballroom, and another, smaller one, at the far end of the hall. John decided to go to the smaller one, telling himself that its out-of-the-way location would, like the corner door, call less attention to himself.

As he stepped out into the hallway, he glanced down toward the main doors and the security guard. The security guard wasn't sitting at his table.

"So much for the hired help," John said under his breath. He walked to the far end of the hall, glancing through the smoked-glass windows at Dallas and beyond. From up here, he had a great view of the city, including the infamous highway interchange known as the Mixmaster where two interstates and the Central Expressway came together. Even though today was Saturday, it was choked with traffic.

Just as John pushed open the door to go into the rest room, a burst of laughter spilled out from the ballroom. "Now, was that laughing because Gil Bates said something funny?" John asked quietly. "Or was that more of the 'Gee, Mr. Bates, you sure are rich' kind of laughter?"

John chuckled at his comment, wishing he had been able to share it with someone.

* * *

Jennifer had just taken a swallow of her punch when a burst of machine-gun fire erupted in the room. The machine-gun fire was followed by screams and shouts of anger and alarm.

"Everyone stay where you are! If you move, you will be shot!" a loud voice called.

Six men rushed into the room, all six armed with AK-47's and all six wearing the traditional Arab headdress.

The two Secret Service agents guarding Mrs. Emerson stepped in front of her, both of them drawing their pistols as they did so. There were two shots, so close together that they sounded like one, and the two agents went down. On one side was a busboy, on the other a caterer. Both were holding smoking pistols, and it was obvious now that they had been planted in the crowd with the specific purpose of taking out the agents. Now, they joined the six armed men who had moved in to take over the room.

"Down, on the floor," the leader of the group said. He made a motion with his hand. "Everyone, sit on the floor. Anyone who stands up will be shot."

Protesting in fear and anger, the crowd began obeying the leader's order. The leader walked up to the front of the room where Bates had been speaking. He took the microphone, then turned to address the room.

"I am Aziz Hassan Faysal, warrior of Allah," he announced to the panic-stricken crowd in the room. "Today the Islamic Jihad Muhahidin has struck a blow at the heart of infidel America."

Four

John was standing at the urinal when he heard the initial burst of gunfire. At almost the same time, he also heard footsteps coming up the hall. Moving quickly into one of the toilet stalls, he stepped up onto the commode, then pulled himself to the top of the partitions. There was a slight depression between the rear of the toilet stall partitions and the wall itself, and John rolled over into that little depression.

Two men came into the rest room. One began kicking open the stall doors, while the other stayed back to check. The one kicking in the doors said something in Arabic.

"Remember, Hakeem, speak only the English," the other cautioned.

"Yes. English," Hakeem replied. He kicked open the last door. "There is no one here."

"I am here," the first man said. He walked over toward the urinal. "And I am going to take a piss now."

"I will wait outside," Hakeem said. He pushed through the door. The remaining Arab leaned his AK-47 against the wall and began relieving himself.

Moving quietly, John put his hands on the edge of the stall. He had to plan his move perfectly because he had to take out the man at the urinal before he had time to call out. He vaulted over the top of the stall, bringing both feet against the side of the Arab's head. The Arab only had time to look up before his lights went out.

With the Arab flat on his back on the concrete floor in front of the urinal, John placed his knee on the terrorist's chest. Putting one hand on the man's chin and the other on the back of his head, he gave a quick jerk. He heard the neck snap.

Grabbing the AK-47, John moved quickly to the door.

"Dawud?" Hakeem called from just outside the door. "What takes you so long to piss? Your cock is not so large that it should take so long." Hakeem laughed at his own joke.

John put his back to the wall and waited. Hakeem opened the door, then stepped inside. He saw Dawud lying on the floor, but was unable to react beyond that because John hit him in the back of the neck with a vicious butt-stroke from the AK-47 he was holding. Hakeem went down, dead before he hit the floor.

Hakeem was carrying a radio, and John picked it up.

"Dawud, Hakeem, where are you?"

John hesitated. Then the voice came over the radio again, a little more insistent this time.

"Hakeem, answer me."

John pressed the talk button. Speaking in a low, gruff voice.

"Toilet. All clear here."

"Very good. Continue the search."

"Yes."

John was glad he was ordered to continue the search rather than rejoin the others. This would buy him a little time to find out what was going on.

The first thing he would have to do, though, was get rid of the two bodies. He did that by moving them into two of the stalls, placing them on the toilets, then using their belts to lift their legs so they couldn't be seen from outside the stall. It wouldn't hold up to a real search, but it would survive a cursory glance into the rest room.

Back in the ballroom, Faysal had his men going through the party guests, collecting cellular telephones. He also had one of his men bring in a TV set. The TV was turned on and the screen was filled with pictures of the attacks that had just been launched against America. Breathless announcers told of the attack at the football stadium in Knoxville, as well as the simultaneous attacks on several of the bridges that crossed the Mississippi River.

"What are you trying to accomplish by these heinous acts?" Bates asked.

"It isn't what we are trying to accomplish, it is what we are accomplishing," he said. "We are going to hurt America where it can be hurt most: in the pocketbook. By this time tomorrow, Mr. Bates, you will be worth considerably less than you are now."

"Our economy is strong," Bates said. "You might cause a ripple, but you can't destroy it. Look at 9/11. We came back from that, we'll come back from this as well."

Faysal laughed. "You don't understand," he said.

"I don't mean you will be poorer because of the stock market. You will be one billion dollars poorer because you are going to make an electronic transfer of that much money to the account of Islamic Jihad Muhahidin."

"You are crazy! One billion dollars, by electronic transfer?"

"Oh, yes," Faysal said. "And the beauty of it is, we will be using software you developed in order to effect that transfer." Faysal pointed to one of his men, who cleared off a place on the buffet table by the simple expedient of raking some of the food onto the floor. He put a laptop computer down on the space that was cleared, opened it, and tapped a few keys. "It's ready for the transfer," Faysal said.

"And if I refuse?"

"Then you will die. But don't feel that we are picking on you only," Faysal said.

He looked around at some of the others, then settled on the face of Carl Tilden. "Ah, Mr. Tilden, owner of Tilden Television Network. You have a great opportunity to reach the world with the truth, Mr. Tilden. Instead, you propagate lies and filth. We will expect two hundred fifty million from you."

One by one, Faysal went to several others, telling each of them the amount of money he expected to be transferred to the account of Islamic Jihad Muhahidin, ending with Jessica Philpot, founder and CEO of Philpot Cosmetics.

"I am an old woman and I can't be frightened by the threat of death," Mrs. Philpot said. "I don't intend to transfer one cent of my money to your heathen cause."

"Yes, Mrs. Philpot, I thought you might react that way. So I intend to use you as an example to the others, just to show that we mean business. You'll understand, I'm sure."

Without fanfare, and doing it so quickly that most didn't realize what was happening until it was over, Faysal raised his pistol and shot Mrs. Philpot in the forehead. Blood gushed from the wound as she fell back amid screams of shock and terror.

Washington, D.C.:

Anticipating some sort of action, Andy Garrison left his home, and was on the way to the office when his cell phone rang.

"Garrison," he said.

"Andy, this is Peter. Call me on a secure line as soon as you can."

"I'm fifteen minutes from the office now," Andy replied.

"Make it in ten," Peter replied.

Nine minutes later Andy called Peter over a secure line. "Is this quick enough for you?" he asked when Peter answered the phone.

"Yes," Peter replied. "On the other hand, it may already be too late. Andy, there's a problem with the First Lady."

"What kind of problem?"

"When the attacks came, the Secret Service tried to contact their agents who were with the First Lady. No response."

"Where is the First Lady?"

"She is in Dallas, at a big reception being given by Gil Bates. We've tried to get through to the agents by satellite phone, and by landline to the tower itself."

"You think the terrorists are after her?"

"Maybe only secondarily," Peter answered. "There are a lot very wealthy people gathered in the DS Towers right now, so with or without Mrs. Emerson, it would be a very attractive target."

"I'll get in immediate touch with our people in Dallas," Andy said.

"Tell them to proceed with caution. We don't want to spook these guys into doing something drastic."

"My God, Peter, what's more drastic than what they've already done? We can't pussyfoot around with these bastards. There's no negotiation, we have to move."

Peter sighed. "Yeah," he said. "I guess you're right."

Senate Office Building:

Senator Harriet Clayton drummed her fingers on her desk and looked at Henry Norton, her Administrative Assistant. "This is awful," she said. "Just awful. All those people killed."

Norton smiled. "Have you ever heard the saying that it is an ill wind that blows no good?"

"Good? What good can come from this?"

"President Emerson has been riding pretty high lately. Believe me, after this, his poll numbers are going to take a big, big hit. And when his numbers go down, our numbers go up."

Harriet shook her head. "No," she said. "I can't attack the President now. Why, the whole country would turn on me."

"You won't be making a direct attack. We'll work out a few statements where you appear to be supporting the President in this time of crisis, while at the same time pointing out the fact that the crisis exists in the first place because his foreign policy is simply unable to address the issues."

"Do you think it will work?" Harriet asked.

"Come on. Have I ever been wrong? Who pulled your ashes out of the fire when your husband got caught sucking that hooker's toes."

"You didn't do much for Eddie. He lost the election."

"I did the only thing I could do, Harriet. I cut the losses. True, he's not the President, but you are a United States Senator."

The door to Harriet's office opened and the appointments secretary stuck her head in. "Senator, your husband is on the phone."

"Thank you," Harriet said.

Harriet had met her husband when they were both students at Harvard. Politically savvy, Harriet helped Eddie get elected to the South Carolina State Senate, then to the governorship. While serving his second term as governor, Edward G. Clayton was tapped by Presidential nominee Jerome Jefferson to run as his Vice President. The Jefferson-Clayton ticket won the election, but it was a tumultuous eight years, dominated by a special prosecutor's investigation of possible financial misdoings on the part of the President.

Clayton had his own scandal when a hooker sold her story about his late-night visits during which the Vice President would suck her toes. Despite that, Eddie Clayton managed to secure the nomination of his party for President, and though his loss was one of the narrowest in history, he did lose.

During the same election in which he lost the Presidency, Harriet Clayton established residency in New Jersey, where she ran a successful campaign for the United States Senate. Some claimed that her campaign for the Senate actually undermined her husband's campaign for the White House. Others pointed out that Harriet's aggressive, acerbic personality was so controversial that he was actually better off without her in his campaign.

Harriet started to pick up the receiver, then punched up the speakerphone instead. "Hello, Eddie," she said.

"Have you heard the latest?" former Vice President Clayton asked. "They've lost contact with the Secret Service agents guarding Karen Emerson." Clayton's voice was rather husky, with a soft, Southern drawl.

"No, I hadn't heard that. Where is she?"

"She's in Dallas. You know, Bates is giving that big party for his new building and she was one of his guests. If you want my guess, terrorists have crashed that party."

"Oh, that's awful," Harriet said.

"Yeah. Well, it comes with the territory. Listen,

what I think you should do is get on the air as quickly as you can," Eddie said. "I'll set it for you, and we'll go on together."

"Eddie, I don't know if it's such a good idea for you two to go on together," Henry said.

There was a beat of silence before the former Vice President replied. "You've got me on speakerphone?"

"Yes, Eddie. Henry is here with me now, we're discussing the best path for me to take."

"I told you the best path for you to take. You need to get on the air and make a comment. I can help you. I was head of Jerry's special task force on terrorism. I've got a good reputation in this field."

"Yes, you do have a good reputation, Eddie. And that's precisely why you should not go on with Harriet," Henry said.

"If you'll excuse me for saying so, Henry, that doesn't make one lick of sense."

"Sure it does. Most people think Harriet got her seat because of you. Your going on with her now will just reinforce that idea."

"Damn it, Henry, I need the exposure. If I don't get back in the public eye soon, and with something important like this, I can kiss getting my party's nomination good-bye forever."

Henry sighed. "I see your point, Eddie, but right now my obligation is to Harriet. You wouldn't want to do anything to damage your wife's career now, would you?"

There was another long beat of silence before Eddie answered. "No. I wouldn't want to do anything like that."

"Good. I knew you would understand. Now, just sit this out for a few days, let Harriet get into it alone, then we'll find some way to bring you on board."

Eddie sighed. "Whatever you say, Henry." It was obvious by the tone of his voice that he wasn't pleased with the idea.

"Thanks, dear. I knew you would understand," Harriet said.

"Yeah," Eddie said again. They heard him hang up.

"Poor Eddie."

"He'll survive," Henry said. "His political career won't, that's already over. But he will survive." Henry smiled. "And you, my dear, will thrive." He began rubbing his hands together in glee. "We couldn't have *asked* for a better situation than this."

Five

When the FBI reached the DS Towers, they discovered that the elevators were inoperative.

"What do we do now, Alex?" one of them asked.

The leader of the FBI team was fourteen-year veteran Alex Kaplan. He looked at the three men who were with him.

"We climb," he said.

Ten minutes later, as the FBI team reached the landing on the thirty-fifth floor, they were suddenly confronted by three armed men. There was a short, savage burst of machine-gun fire, and Alex and all three of his men went down.

Even from the sixty-sixth floor, John could hear the machine-gun fire. Some may not have recognized it for what it was, for it was faint and indistinct. But John had heard machine-gun fire many times, and in many places, so it was not something he would mistake.

Shortly after the distant gunfire, a message popped over the radio.

"Faysal, this is Kadar. The intruders were FBI. We killed all of them."

"Very good, Kadar," Faysal replied. "Continue to search the building. Kill anyone you see."

"In the name of Allah," Kadar said.

"In the name of Allah," Faysal repeated.

Turning the volume down, John moved up the hall toward the ballroom, staying close to the wall. Just as he reached the door he had used to exit the ballroom, someone came out. Because the man was dressed exactly as Dawud and Hakeem had been dressed, John knew immediately that this was one of the terrorists. The man flashed a momentary expression of surprise as he came face-to-face with John Barrone. Using the AK-47 he was now carrying, John took the terrorist down with a vertical butt-stroke to the chin.

Knowing he couldn't leave him lying in the hallway, John grabbed him by the collar of his shirt and started dragging him away. At first he was going to take him all the way back to the men's room, but as he passed the elevator bank, he got an idea. Stepping up to one of the elevators, he managed to force the doors open far enough to push the terrorist through. How far the terrorist fell, John had no idea, but it was so far that John didn't hear him hit bottom.

As John turned away from the elevator, he saw Don Yee slipping out of the ballroom through the same door.

"Don!" John whispered harshly. He waved at him. "Down here!"

John led Don back into the rest room.

"How are the women?"

"They're fine," Don said. "They covered for me while I slipped out."

"Is there any chance they can get out too?"

"I think so. Right now this fellow Faysal is concentrating on the people who have the money. By the way, we were taking odds on whether or not you were still alive."

"Yeah? Who voted against me?"

"Well, all three of us," Don said, smiling. "But we were hoping we were wrong."

"How many are in there?"

"There are eight inside—the leader, whose name is Faysal, and seven others, including two, a busboy and a caterer, who were plants. Actually, there *were* seven others, but one of them left a moment before I did."

"Yes, I saw him leave."

"Where did he go, do you know?"

"He went downstairs," John replied. "He must have been in a hurry, though, he didn't bother to wait for the elevator." John made a dropping motion with his hand.

At first, Don was confused. Then he smiled. "You helped him, I'm sure."

"What are friends for?"

"How many more are out here, do you know?" Don asked.

John held up the radio. "I'm not sure, but I do know they have people roaming around," he said. "I heard shooting a few minutes ago, then someone reported in that they had killed an FBI team."

"Damn," Don said.

"At least word is out about what is happening here," John said.

"Yes, well, what's happening here isn't happening just here," Don said.

"What do you mean? Are they holding another building somewhere?"

"Worse. An A-10 attacked a packed football field in Knoxville, Tennessee, killing hundreds. And they've knocked out all, or nearly all, of the bridges across the Mississippi River."

"Ambitious bastards, aren't they? Well, we'd better do what we can to break this up."

Opening the door slightly, John looked out into the hall and, seeing no one, motioned for Don to come on. As they moved down the hallway, the elevator dinged and the doors started to open.

"In here," John said, pushing open the nearest door. The two of them stepped inside while John stared through a crack in the door.

"See anything?" Don asked.

"Yes," John answered. "I figured they had taken control of the elevators and I was right. I'm sure this is the group that killed the FBI men."

"We're in the stairwell," Don said. He looked up. "I thought we were on the top floor. This is as high as the elevators come. What's up there?"

"I don't know. Sometimes the public elevators don't run all way to the top floor."

"Let's see what's up there," Don suggested.

The two men climbed the flight of stairs, then opened the door at the top. The door opened onto a hallway. Next to the door was an elevator, though it was much smaller than the public elevators, and instead of a call button, there was a key receptacle.

"Just as I thought," John said. "A private elevator."

Across the hall from the elevator was a large area with reclining chairs, tables, and potted palms. The ceiling, and most of the walls, were of smoked glass.

"Must be a place where the executives come to relax," John said. He started walking around, then stopped and jerked back.

"What is it?" Don asked.

"A skylight that looks down into the ballroom," John said.

Getting down to lessen the chances of being seen, the two men crawled up to the edge of the skylight, then looked through it at the room below. They could see the guests, sitting uncomfortably on the floor, while armed guards moved around keeping an eye on them. They could also see three bodies stretched out, one woman, and two men.

"They killed Mrs. Emerson's Secret Service agents right away," Don said.

"Who's the woman?"

"That's Mrs. Philpot, the cosmetic queen. She as much as told them to kiss her ass, she wasn't giving them a cent. Faysal decided to use her as an example, so he shot her."

"Brave woman," John said. "What's going on there?" he asked, pointing to someone sitting at a computer.

"Money transfers," Don answered. "Faysal has demanded that everyone in the room make an electronic transfer of money from their accounts to some terrorist account."

"Why are they doing it?"

"He threatened to kill them if they don't. That was the point he was making with Mrs. Philpot."

"Yes, well, the point is, he will probably kill them all anyway if we don't stop it."

"You have any ideas yet on how we're going to do that?"

"Not yet," John answered. "I was sort of hoping something would come to me by now."

John and Don scooted back away from the skylight, then stood up and looked around. At the rear of the lounge was another door.

"I wonder where that goes," Don said.

"Only one way to find out," John said. He started toward the door and Don followed him. Pushing through the door, they went inside. The room was large, well-lit, and filled with computer terminals.

"Wow," Don said. "Look at this array of computers."

"Well, this is the world headquarters for Dyna-Systems," John said. "What did you expect?"

"Couldn't I have fun in a place like this," Don said. Don was a computer genius who, under different circumstances, might have been a Bill Gates or a Gil Bates.

"Yes, I suppose you could," John replied.

"Hey, John, I'd like to try something."

"What?"

"This guy Faysal is having everyone down there make computer transfers of large sums of money to their account, right? Well I think I can stop that."

John knew that if anyone could reverse what was going on down there now, Don could.

"Give it a try," John said.

Don sat at one of the terminals, tapped a few keys, and a moment later, smiled broadly. "I knew it!" he said. "They're going through the DynaSystems mainframe. I can monitor everything they are doing from here."

Don began tapping keys.

"Can you get in?"

"Yeah. In fact, it's too damn easy. I need some sort of challenge."

"Challenge?"

"Yeah." Don tapped a few more keys, then chuckled. "Hey, how is the Code Team on operating expenses?"

"I don't know, why? You aren't planning to give us the money, are you?"

"Yes."

"Good try, Don, but I don't think . . . ,"

"Look, the market is going to take a hit, right? You remember what happened after the planes flew into the WTC?"

"Yes."

"When the market bottoms on Monday, I'll buy. So far I've transferred three hundred million dollars into in an interest-bearing money account until Monday. In addition, I've closed out the source account where this money was going. That's another ten million dollars. On Monday, I'll track the Dow for twenty-four hours, then return the money to its sources by close of business on Tuesday. That will stabilize the market and keep the country from going into another slide." Don grinned broadly. "And any profit we might make will go directly into the Code Name account.

We should pick up about a nice piece of change in the transaction."

"Damn," John said. "You're handy to have . . ." John's comment was interrupted by someone coming into the room. It was one of the terrorists.

"Who are you?"

"We're janitors," John replied.

"Janitors wearing clothes like that? I don't think so."

John had put his weapon down, and couldn't get to it now without arousing the terrorist's suspicion.

"Well, you know how Mr. Bates is," John said. "He likes for all of his employees to be well dressed."

Don continued to tap on the computer.

"You!" the terrorist said, pointing to Don. "What are you doing? Get away from there!"

Don pushed the enter button, completing his operation, then stood up.

"Outside," the terrorist said, underscoring his order with a wave of his weapon. It was then that he noticed the AK-47 John had put down. Quickly, he raised his own rifle to his shoulder and pointed it at John. "How did you get that gun?" he asked.

"I don't know," John said. "It was here when we came in."

"Outside!" the terrorist said again.

Raising their hands, John and Don walked outside, with the terrorist following close behind. John walked straight toward the skylight and the terrorist, watching both John and Don closely, didn't notice where they were going. When they reached the edge of the skylight, they stopped.

"Why did you stop? Keep going!" the terrorist

ordered. To enforce his order, he stepped up close to them. That was his mistake, for as soon as he did, John leaped to one side and Don to the other.

For a moment, the terrorist was confused, unsure of which one to go after. That moment of confusion cost him dearly, for both John and Don pivoted around on one leg, while bringing the other up to strike a blow. The terrorist was hit in the back by powerful kicks from both John and Don. With a shout of alarm, he pitched forward, crashing through the skylight.

A remote area of Sitarkistan:

In a remote and mountainous area of Sitarkistan, a network of interconnecting caves and tunnels was home for Abdul Kadan Kadar. The cave entrances could not be seen by satellite because rock overhangs protected them from overhead observation. They could not be seen by aerial surveillance because the entrances were skillfully covered with camouflage netting that was the same color as the rocks and sand surrounding the site.

They couldn't even be seen from the ground until one was very close. Then one could also see, in addition to the well-guarded cave entrances, camouflaged vehicles, an array of downlinks and antennae, a generator—which was currently running—two heavy machine-gun emplacements, and a cadre of armed and patrolling guards. This was the headquarters of the Islamic Jihad Muhahidin.

Abdul Kadan Kadar, the leader of the Islamic

Jihad Muhahidin, had taken the largest chamber as his personal headquarters, and though the other cave chambers were meanly furnished and over-crowded with men, Kadar had managed to turn his personal quarters into a palace. The inside walls of his cave were draped with yellow, green, and black silk. A fine carpet was on the dirt floor and exquis-itely carved tables were scattered about. On one of the tables was displayed a silver tea-service set.

Kadar was sitting on a large pillow, sipping tea as he watched a video of the attacks in America. The video had been taken from images telecast world-wide by World Satellite Network. Among the array of downlinks was a disc that could tune in to WSN's television signals, as well as signals from dozens of other television broadcast facilities. Kadar's com-munication network was absolutely state-of-the-art. Although he was in one of the most remote areas of the world, he could, with a few simple taps on the computer keyboard, or merely by picking up a satellite phone, connect with anyone, anywhere, anytime.

"Tell me, Farid, who was the pilot of the plane that attacked the sports stadium?" Kadar asked.

"His name was Abdullah Afif Akil," Farid replied.

"And how is it that he was able to use one of the U.S. Air Force's own planes against them?"

Farid laughed. "That is the best part of it, Imam. Abdullah was a lieutenant in the Sitarkistan Air Force. He was in the United States for flight train-ing in the A-10."

Kadar reached for a cookie. "I see. The airplane he was flying today was an A-10, was it not?"

"Yes, Imam."

"Then he learned well."

"Yes, Imam."

"And the U.S. Government paid for it?"

"They did."

Kadar laughed out loud. "That is very funny." He held up his index finger. "Many do not realize it, Farid, but Allah does enjoy a joke. This is proof of that."

"Yes, Imam."

"His name was Abdullah Afif Akil?"

"Yes."

"Then I shall say a prayer for him," Kadar said. Going to his knees, Kadar put his hands out, then lowered his head to the ground. He was quiet for a moment, then raised up and retook his seat on the pillow.

"I have asked that Abdulla Afif Akil be granted entrance into paradise, but the words of man mean little. It is only the action of Allah the Pure, Allah the Magnificent, who can grant entry into heaven. But surely, this brave young man is with Allah now."

"What are the Americans doing about our attacks against them?" Kadar asked.

"The Americans can do nothing," Farid said.

Kadar laughed, and pointed to the screen. The video was at the point where the A-10 was flying directly toward the camera. "Look how the Americans photographed their own death."

"By now, all Americans have seen this same picture many times," Farid said. "They are so foolish, they do not understand that by showing the act of our brave young warrior, and the death and destruction of their people, they are undermining their own will to resist. Allah will grant us ultimate victory over the infidels."

"And Azil? What have we heard from him? Is everything going as planned?"

"Yes, all is going as planned," Farid answered. "He has taken control of the building and has begun transferring money to our account."

"Think what we can do with one billion dollars," Kadar said.

"The infidels of the world will know and fear the name Abdul Kadan Kadar," Farid said.

"Let us see how things are going," Kadar suggested, pointing toward the computer.

Nodding, Farid moved over to the computer. It was on a table and Farid, who had been sitting on a pillow on the floor, now sat on a chair in order to access the computer. He logged on.

"I am pleased to report that already half a billion dollars have been transferred to our account," Farid said, smiling broadly.

"Allah be praised."

"Wait. There is more," Farid said, holding up his finger. "Now there is . . . ," Farid stopped and stared at the screen. His smile froze in place, then turned to a look of confusion. "I do not understand," he said.

"What is it?" Kadar asked.

"No, this cannot be," Farid said. He pointed to the screen. "The money is being taken out."

"What?"

"The money that was put into our account is being taken out," Farid said. "And not only *that* money, *our* money as well." Farid looked at Kadar with an expression of disbelief on his face.

"No, you are mistaken," Kadar said, hurrying quickly over to the computer.

"See for yourself," Farid said, pointing to the screen.

Kadar watched as the money was taken from his account and transferred elsewhere.

"Stop it! Stop this from happening!" Kadar shouted.

Desperately, Farid began tapping keys, trying to get into the bank to override the command that was draining the account. Nothing he tried worked, and the two men watched in horror as the little graph bar continue to slide across the screen, showing the process of the transaction. Finally, the bar was blue all the way across. An information box came onto the screen. "All funds have been withdrawn. The account is at zero," the information in the box read.

Kadar screamed out in rage, then picked up the computer and threw it to the ground. "It is Faysal!" Kadar said, spittle coming from his mouth. "He has stolen all the money for his own use! I will kill him for this!"

Six

Andy Garrison and Peter Simmons were in the Oval Office of the White House. Also present was Stu Phillips, National Security Advisor, and President Emerson. Emerson was standing behind his desk, staring through the window out toward the Rose Garden.

"I wonder how many Presidents have stood in this very spot, staring through this very window, whenever something like this has happened," Emerson said.

"Every President since Theodore Roosevelt, I imagine," Andy said. "He was the first to use the Oval Office."

"I expect so," Emerson replied. He sighed. "I think of people like Woodrow Wilson during the First World War, Roosevelt and Truman during World War II, and LBJ and Nixon during Vietnam. Even Bush, after the World Trade Center." Emerson turned away from the window and looked at the three men who were with him. "But damn it, man, did any of them have to consider the fact that their wife was being held hostage by madmen? If she is a hostage. She may not even be alive."

"Mr. President, we have no reason to think that she has been killed," Peter said.

"On the contrary," Andy added. "It would be counterproductive for them to kill her."

Emerson shook his head, then pinched the bridge of his nose. "Counterproductive assumes a certain degree of rationality," he said. "And I pray that you are right. But we already know these people aren't rational." He sighed. "What is our latest casualty count?"

"The numbers from the football field aren't solid, but we think there were four hundred and twelve killed there."

"And on the bridges?"

"That's a little more difficult to discern. There were some cars dropped into the water, and all of them haven't been recovered. But our best estimate for all the bridges is one hundred twenty-seven."

"And in Dallas?"

"The only casualties we are sure of are the four FBI men who were killed."

"Have we made contact with the terrorists?"

"No, sir. We've been trying to contact them, but they have shut down the phone system."

"What about cell phones? Surely someone in that crowd was carrying a cell phone."

"We've gathered up as many cell-phone numbers as we could and we are trying to call them as well, but so far, no luck. Evidently the terrorists collected all the cell phones as soon as they hit."

"So what you are saying is we are stalemated? We

are at the whim and mercy of whoever did this?" Emerson asked.

"Yes, sir," Peter said. "I'm afraid so."

"There is one thing," Andy said. He held up his finger. "It's a long shot but . . ."

"But what?" President Emerson said.

Andy cleared his throat, then looked at Peter Emerson and Stu Phillips. "I wonder if you gentlemen could excuse us for a moment."

"I'm cleared for . . ." Stu began, but Peter interrupted him.

"Come with me, Stu. I've got something I want to talk to you about anyway."

Stu looked at the President, who, with a slight nod of his head, indicated that Stu should leave. Reluctantly, Stu followed Peter out of the Oval Office. Andy waited until he heard the door click shut before he turned back to the President.

"Now, what is it that is so secret that neither the FBI nor my Chief of Staff can hear it?" Emerson asked.

"Mr. President, there are four members of the Code Name Team at that party."

It was obvious by the expression on Emerson's face that he didn't know what Andy was talking about. "The Code Name Team?" he asked. He shook his head. "Who, or what, is the Code Name Team?"

"The Code Name Team is an organization whose job is to take care of things that fall through the cracks, things that, for one reason or another, the government can't handle through its regular agencies," Andy explained. "They have no government connection. Indeed, since they are extralegal, they are sometimes at cross-purposes with the government. On the other hand, there are some of us within the government who know about the team."

"And you say they were present at the Bates reception?"

"Yes, sir. Well, some of them are anyway. I'm not sure how many are there, but I do know for a fact that John Barrone is there."

"Who is John Barrone?"

"He is the leader of the team. He spent twenty-two years with the CIA. Some of the older hands over at the CIA speak very highly of him."

"What is their operating authority?" President Emerson asked.

"They can function under the auspices of a private detective agency, a private security firm, or a bail-bonding operation . . . whatever it takes to give them the cover they need."

"If they are that secret, how on earth did they ever get funding through the Congress?"

Andy smiled. "That's the beauty of it, Mr. President. They are privately funded."

"Privately funded? That means no governmental control of any kind?"

"None, sir."

"So what you are telling me is that our only hope in Dallas depends upon a bunch of renegades, a loose cannon on deck, as it were."

Andy nodded. "Yes, sir, that's what I'm telling you. But this loose cannon packs a pretty good wallop. In fact, I wouldn't be surprised if they had already fired their first volley."

* * *

The DS Towers in Dallas:

To the surprise of everyone in the ballroom, there was a sudden drop-in guest. The terrorist who had encountered John and Don in the lounge area above now came crashing through the overhead skylight, onto the buffet table. The impact of his fall caused the table to collapse, and he lay on his back, sprawled out on the petit-four tray, a large, jagged, and bloody shard of glass protruding through his chest.

Nearly everyone in the room reacted to the sudden drop-in, including Faysal. Looking up, he saw two faces staring down at him through the skylight, and with a shout of rage, he raised his AK-47 and began firing, emptying his magazine. Following his example, the other guards began firing as well, and for several seconds, the room reverberated with the staccato crash of gunfire. The ejected shell casings tumbled everywhere and bullets smashed through the skylight, or ricocheted off the steel frame. The guests, who were still sitting on the floor, screamed in alarm and put their hands in their ears, then leaned forward, putting their heads between their legs.

"Now," Jennifer said to Linda. "Before they can reload."

Quickly, Linda and Jennifer slipped through the same door that John and Don had used earlier. In the confusion, no one even saw them leave.

The two women were spotted in the hall, though,

because one of the rovers Faysal had sent out was coming back to check on the shooting. Seeing Jennifer and Linda, he shouted and brought his gun up.

"Halt!" he yelled.

Both women stopped.

"Where are you going?" the terrorist asked, coming toward them.

"I'm going to the ladies' room," Jennifer said.

"I'm going with her," Linda said.

"It takes two of you?"

Jennifer smiled. "You don't know American women very well, do you? We never go to the ladies' room alone."

"Get back inside," the terrorist said. He emphasized his statement by waving his gun toward the door. The waving action of his gun caused the muzzle to move away so that it was no longer aimed directly at them. That action was all the opening Jennifer and Linda needed. Reacting in unison, as if the move had been choreographed, Jennifer continued to push the weapon to one side while Linda sent a well-aimed kick to the terrorist's groin. Relaxing his grip on the gun, the terrorist doubled over in pain. Jennifer jerked the gun away, then brought it up under his chin in a vertical butt-stroke that snapped his head back and put him down.

"Upstairs!" Jennifer said, starting for the stairwell. Linda followed, and the two women ran up the stairs.

"John! Don, it's us!" Jennifer shouted when they reached the top of the stairs.

The door jerked open and John and Don were standing there, waiting for them.

"I see you got our invitation," John said.

"Yes. I must say you used a rather unique way to deliver it."

"We'd better get ready," Linda said. "Faysal will be sending people up here."

Suddenly the windows were shattered by machine-gun fire coming from outside the building.

"Get down!" John shouted, diving for the floor.

A helicopter was hovering just outside the window, and two men dressed in black were sitting in the open door of the Jet Ranger, spraying machine-gun fire into the room. The bullets crashed into the potted plants and snapped through the rattan chairs of the lounge.

"Hey, wait, that's our guys!" Don shouted. He stood up and tried to wave, but the whistling bullets made him drop down again.

"Damn! They're shooting at the wrong people!"

"You can't blame them," John said. "How can they tell the difference?"

Suddenly, even as they were watching, a rocket-propelled grenade, fired from somewhere up on the roof of the building, streamed into the heli-copter. The grenade detonated, and the helicopter began spinning as it went down.

John ran over to the window and looked out. The pilot managed to regain control of the heli-copter, establishing an auto-rotation to the street below. The street was filled with police cars, scores of them, all with flashing red and blue lights. In ad-dition to the police cars, there were fire trucks, ambulances, and armored personnel carriers.

"It looks like we're going to have company," John

said. "I'd say every SWAT team in the state of Texas is down there now. Hope they have better luck than the first group did."

"Oh, I hope they don't try and come up the stairs," Linda said.

"Why not?"

"I heard them talking. They've got bombs rigged in the stairwells."

At that moment the door burst open and four terrorists rushed in, firing their AK-47's. The terrorists had no specific targets, and were just firing indiscriminately. On the other hand, John, Don, and Jenny had easy targets because the terrorists were bunched together at the door. When John, Don, and Jenny opened fire, the intruders went down quickly.

John stood there for a moment, looking at the men who had just burst in on them. Then he clicked on the radio he had been carrying. "Faysal," he said.

"Who is this?" Faysal's voice replied.

"Well, you might call me Satan," John replied. "Because I'm bringing you hell."

"Blasphemer! You will die!"

"We're all going to die, asshole. It's just that some will die before others. These four, for example."

"What four?"

"Hold on, I'll send them down."

John, Don, Jennifer, and Linda pulled the four bodies over to the broken skylight.

"Are you ready for them?" John asked on the radio.

"I do not understand," said Faysal.

"Heads up," John said. He nodded his head to the others, and they pushed all four bodies through the skylight. Even from up there, they could hear the crash of the bodies as they hit the floor below.

"Devil! Devil!" Faysal shouted. "You are a devil!" Then, to what rovers he had remaining, he screamed out orders. "Find the devil! Find him and kill him!"

"There's more than one of them, Faysal," one of the rovers replied.

"Then find all of them and kill them all!" Faysal demanded loudly.

John chuckled, then turned off the radio. "I guess we'd better find another place to be," he said.

"Where do we go?" Don asked. "And how do we get there?"

"I don't know where, but we're going to have to take the stairs. Jennifer, did you hear where the bombs were placed in the stairwell?"

"Not exactly," Jennifer replied. "But my guess would be about four or five stories below."

"Then we should be able to get at least one floor below Faysal without too much trouble," John said. "Let's go."

Seven

On the streets surrounding
the DS Tower Building:

Chief Keith Collins had set up his command post at the corner of Clarence and Singer Streets. From this position, he had a view of the building from its northwest corner to its southeast corner. He had watched with the others as the helicopter came spiraling down, the pilot barely managing to regain control in time to land safely. The pilot, copilot, and four of the assault team were wounded by the grenade blast. Two of the assault team were killed.

Now, Collins was standing just outside his car, talking on the cell phone to Andy Garrison in Washington.

"I know the President's wife is in there, Mr. Garrison," Chief Collins was saying into the phone. "Do you think the First Lady could come to Dallas and I would not know about it? We're doing everything we can. But just so that you know, we'd be doing everything we could whether Mrs. Emerson was in there or not."

"I'm sure you would, Chief," Andy said. "I just

wanted to make sure you were fully apprised of the situation there."

"Trust me, I am fully apprised."

"Chief," one of the other policemen called.

"Look, Mr. Garrison, I'll keep Homeland Security posted on everything that's going on here as well as I can. But I hope you understand that at the moment I'm pretty busy. I have to go." He punched the phone off without saying good-bye, then looked toward the policeman who had called to him.

"Yes, Miller, what is it?"

"The assault teams have reached the fifty-fifth floor in both the north and south stairwells."

"No resistance encountered?"

"None, sir."

"All right, tell them to continue on up. But be careful. Remember what happened to the FBI guys."

"Right."

"I still say we should put an assault team on the roof," one of the others said.

"We tried that. We got two men killed and nearly lost everyone on the helicopter."

"That's because we didn't know about the RPG on the roof. We know about it now, and we can deal with it."

"How are we going to deal with it?" Chief Collins asked.

"That's easy. We'll just make a few passes with armed helicopters, and shoot the place up."

"Shoot the place up?" Collins asked.

"Yeah, nothing to it."

"Correct me if I'm wrong, but the ballroom

where this party was being held is just one floor below the roof."

"Yes, but I don't see what that has to do with it."

"It has everything to do with it. Unless you can give me a one-hundred-percent guarantee that nobody on that floor will be hurt. Can you give me that guarantee, Marvin?"

"Well, no," Marvin replied. "Nobody could give you a one-hundred-percent guarantee."

"Then there will be no air strike against the roof."

The conversation between Chief Collins and Marvin was interrupted by a heavy, stomach-shaking explosion. A large fireball erupted from the northwest corner of the building, followed by a billowing cloud of smoke.

"My God! They've blown up the building!" someone shouted.

"Take it easy, take it easy!" Chief Collins shouted. "They haven't blown up the whole building. Just . . . damn, that's the stairwell. Who's in there?"

"Captain Dixon is in that one, Lieutenant Kirby is in the south stairwell."

"Call Kirby."

"Don't you mean Dixon?"

Collins shook his head. "It's too late for Dixon. Call Kirby, tell him to back out of there, now!"

"Kirby. Kirby, do you hear me?"

"We're at fifty-seven," Kibry's voice replied. The exertion of the rapid, fast climb could be heard in his voice.

"Stop," Kirby was called. "Stop now."

"Say again? Did you say stop?"

"That's affirmative. Don't move one more step. Hold on for Chief Collins."

Collins reached for the phone. "Lieutenant Kirby, this is Chief Collins."

"Yes, Chief."

"A bomb just went off in the north stairwell. I'm sure there's one on your side as well."

"Want us to try and find it?"

"No. I want you to come back down."

"I beg your pardon, Chief. Did you say you wanted us to come back down?"

"That is affirmative. I want you to come back now. We'll have to come up with some other way. Do you hear me? Come back down."

"Chief, we're nearly there, we could . . ."

"Come back down now! That's an order!"

"Ten-four," Kirby answered.

"What are we going to do now?" Marvin asked.

Collins sighed. "You tell me and we'll both know."

"Chief!" someone called. "Chief, you might want to hear this." The person who called to him, a woman officer, was sitting in a van in front of a shelf full of radio equipment.

"What is it, Shirley? What's going on?"

"We've isolated their radio frequency," Shirley said. "We can listen in on their conversations." Shirley turned a knob, and everyone around the van could hear what was going on.

"They are not here, Faysal. We have searched everywhere."

"Find them!" Faysal demanded. "Find them! I

want Satan found and brought to me. And I want him alive so I can kill him myself."

"Sounds like Faysal is having problems," Marvin said.

"Faysal," a clearly American voice said.

"I wonder who this is," Collins said.

"Not another American traitor, I hope," Marvin replied.

"Faysal, this is Satan," the American voice said. "How many more clowns do you have looking for me? I've killed eight of them. You must be running pretty low on manpower by now."

"He's killed eight of the terrorists?" Chief Collins said. "Who *is* this guy?"

Marvin and Shirley shook their heads, indicating that they had no idea who it was.

"I'm not going to send anyone else after you," Faysal said. "You are going to come in and give yourself up."

"Now, why would I want to do that?"

"Because I am going to start killing hostages if you do not. I will kill one every minute, until you do come in."

"Okay, start killing them."

"I am serious. I have already killed many times, and I will kill again, unless you and your friends give yourselves up."

"No deal. Start killing."

"Are you crazy? What kind of law officer are you that you would say such a thing?"

"I *am* crazy, and I'm *not* a law officer. Kill as many as you want, it's no skin off my ass. Just so that you know I'm coming for you, Faysal. And if you are the only one left alive by the time I get to you, that's fine with me."

"Give me that mike," Chief Collins said, reaching for a microphone. He keyed the talk switch. "To the person calling himself Satan, this is Chief Collins of the Dallas Police Department. Would you identify yourself, please?"

"I'd rather not do that. Faysal is calling me Satan. If you want to talk to me, just call me Satan."

"What are you doing up there, Satan?"

"I'm killing terrorists. And I plan to keep on killing them until they are all gone."

"Are you with some law-enforcement agency?"

"No, I'm not with anyone. I'm just sort of having fun, you might say."

"Having fun?" Chief Collins said, nearly choking on the words.

"Oh, yeah. I'm having a blast."

"You are aware that the President's wife is among the hostages, aren't you?"

"So I've been told."

"You say you are aware, and yet, when Faysal threatened to start killing, you told him to go ahead."

"Like I told the man, Chief. Whoever he kills is no sweat off my ass. He can kill as many as he wants to kill. Hell, he can start with the First Lady as far as I'm concerned. I didn't vote for Emerson for President."

"Perhaps you had better stand down and let the police handle this," Collins suggested.

"Yeah, I can see what a great job you've done so far," John said sarcastically.

"Chief, it's Washington calling again," one of Collins's men said.

"Tell them I'm busy."

"You might want to talk to this person," the policeman said.

"What makes you think so?" Collins asked.

"Because this is the President."

Sighing, Collins walked over to take the telephone. "This is Chief Collins," he said.

"Chief Collins, hold, please, for the President of the United States."

Collins held the phone for a second, then heard the familiar voice of the President. "Chief, this is Bill Emerson."

"Yes, Mr. President."

"I know you've got quite a situation on your hands right now, and I want you to know that the whole country is watching and praying for you."

"Thank you, sir."

"I understand you've lost some of your officers."

"Yes, sir, I have."

"I would appreciate it if, as soon as you have the information, you would get their names to me. I want to personally call their families, thank them for the heroic efforts of their loved ones, and offer my condolences for their loss."

"Yes, Mr. President, I'll do that."

"What is happening right now? I'm watching the news on TV, but I'd like your insight."

"There have been four attempted assaults, Mr. President, one by the FBI and three by us. The FBI assault was stopped first, then the terrorists shot down our helicopter, and another attempt was stopped by a bomb in the stairwell. We called the last assault back for fear they would run into a bomb as well."

"Good for you, Chief, that was the thing to do. I want these evil bastards stopped, but I would like to do so without losing any more lives."

"Mr. President, I know your wife is in there and . . ."

"I'm concerned about her of course," the President said, interrupting Chief Collins. "But I'm concerned for everyone, and I'm especially concerned for the safety of your men."

"Yes, sir, I appreciate that, sir," Chief Collins said. "Oh, there is one possible problem that has come up. A fly in the ointment, so to speak."

"A fly in the ointment?"

"Yes, sir. Evidently there is some cowboy up there who must've been a guest at the party. I don't know how he did it, or quite what is going on, but somehow he seems to have gotten away and is now killing off the terrorists one by one. He has killed eight of them so far."

There was a beat of silence from the other end before the President spoke again. "Do you know his name?"

"No, sir, he wouldn't give me his name. That is, beyond Satan."

"Satan?"

"That's what Faysal is calling him."

"Who is Faysal?"

"I think he is the leader of the terrorists. Faysal is the only name we have for him at this point."

"Well, if this fella Satan is killing terrorists, I say that's good. Don't interfere with him."

"But Mr. President, he's a cowboy. He's not under anyone's control."

"You said he has killed eight of the terrorists, right?"

"Yes, sir. I have no way of confirming that, of course, but he claims to have killed eight of them and Faysal doesn't dispute it. In fact, Faysal's comments seems to validate the claim."

"Are you in communication with Faysal?" The President asked.

"Not really. We have tried to communicate with him, but Faysal won't answer any of our direct questions. However, this man who calls himself Satan seems to have taken one of the terrorists' radios and he and Faysal are communicating. We are now monitoring their communications."

"Continue to do so. At the moment, this . . . Satan . . . person may be the only thing we have going for us," President Emerson said.

"There's one more thing," Collins said.

"What is that?"

Collins was going to tell the President about Faysal's threat to start killing off the hostages, and of Satan's reply, but lost his nerve.

"You say there is one more thing?" President Emerson asked when Collins didn't respond.

"Nothing, sir," Collins said. "I'll pull my men back and let Satan do whatever he can do."

There was no need, Collins decided, to worry the President any more than he was already worried. Besides, if Faysal did start killing people, he was sure he would save the Presidenat's wife until near the end. Despite all the wealthy guests at the party, it was the First Lady who would have the most bargaining power with the U.S. Government.

Washington, D.C., the Oval Office:

"You heard?" President Emerson asked as he hung up the phone. Andy Garrison had been listening in on another line.

"Yes, Mr. President."

"This fellow, Satan. Do you think he is one of the Code Name people you were telling me about?"

"I'm sure of it. I would bet the farm that it is John Barrone," Andy said.

"I hope he is as good as you say he is."

"He is the best."

"And he used to be with the CIA, you say?"

"Yes, sir."

"If he is as good as you say he is, why did we let him get away?"

"We can't afford him."

"There are ways of raising money beyond normal budgets," President Emerson said. "I mean, if he gets results."

"I'm not talking about money," Andy said. "It's the way he gets those results that we can't afford. Politically, if you know what I mean."

"Yes, I know what you mean," President Emerson said. He picked up a small, black swagger stick and tapped it lightly into the palm of his left hand. This was his "Garry Owen" stick, the same stick he had carried when he was a lieutenant with the Seventh Cavalry in Vietnam. "But right now I would resign my office just for the opportunity to see this man Faysal skinned alive."

Eight

When one of the studio employees came into the green room, Harriet called out to her.

"Young lady?"

"Yes, Senator Clayton?" The young employee had her arms full of file folders, and she had to use her chin to help hold them all in place.

"I'd like a cup of coffee, please, with cream, no sugar," Harriet said.

The coffee server was right next to Harriet's chair, and the studio employee looked pointedly at it, then at Harriet.

"You want me to get you a cup of coffee?"

"Look, I know you are an hourly-wage employee, but I wouldn't think a simple thing like getting a United States Senator a cup of coffee would tax your limited abilities beyond reason," Harriet said, sneering.

"No, I think I can handle it," the young woman replied. Looking around the room, she found a place to put down her load of file folders. "Cream, no sugar?"

"Yes," Harriet said. "I know it's confusing, both are white. But the cream is liquid."

"Yes, ma'am."

The young woman drew a cup of coffee, then poured in some cream and handed it to Harriet. Harriet was so busy watching the television screen than she didn't even bother to offer a thank-you.

On screen, Douglas Sharbell, who had achieved some notoriety for conducting an in-depth and somewhat sympathetic interview with Osama Bin Laden back when he was being hunted by the United States, was now reporting on the latest incidents of terror.

"Yes, these terror attacks are bad, and from our perspective, the terrorists themselves are evil," Sharbell said. He leaned toward the camera. "But I ask you to consider this. For some time now, we in the United States have conducted our foreign policy as if we were the masters and all the rest of the world our slaves. We have left an enormous and ugly footprint upon the world, and as a journalist who has traveled far and wide, I can tell you that our presence has not always been welcome.

"Is it any wonder then that the fastest-growing religion in the world feels pressured by American policy? Until we find some way to show others that we want to be partners with the rest of the world, and not masters of it, we are going to face these admittedly terrible, but understandable, acts of desperation.

"Here is an example of what I am talking about. Abdul Kadan Kadar, leader of the Islamic Jihad Muhahidin, the organization that has claimed responsibility for the attacks at Knoxville, and on the bridges across the Mississippi River, as well as the ongoing situation in Dallas, has issued a fatwa. The fatwa is an insight into what drives the man, but so far, not one television broadcasting company in America will carry it. I am pleased to announce that World Satellite News will present Mr. Kadar's fatwa. A fatwa, as some of you may know, is a religious order, given by a leader who commands the respect of Muslims the world over. Once issued, it must be carried out by all who believe for, in the Islamic faith, a fatwa carries the same power as an edict directly from Allah."

Although the fatwa was printed on the teleprompter, Sharbell put on a pair of rimless glasses, then picked up a sheet of paper and began to read.

"'Praise be to Allah, who revealed the book, controls the clouds, defeats factionalism, and says in his book: "But when the forbidden months are past, then fight and slay the pagans wherever ye find them, seize them, beleaguer them, and lie in wait for them in every stratagem of war." Peace be upon our Prophet, Muhammad Bin Abdallah, who said: "I have been sent with the sword between my hands to ensure that no one but Allah is worshipped, Allah who put my livelihood under the shadow of my spear and who inflicts humiliation and scorn on those who disobey my orders."

"'The ruling to kill the Americans and their allies—civilians and military—is an individual duty for every Muslim who can do it in any country in which it is possible to do it, in order to liberate the Al-Aqsa

Mosque and the holy mosque of Mecca from their grip, and in order for their armies to move out of all the lands of Islam, defeated and unable to threaten any Muslim. This is in accordance with the words of Almighty Allah, "and fight the pagans all together as they fight you all together," and "fight them until there is no more tumult or oppression, and there prevails justice and faith in Allah."

"'We—with Allah's help—call on every Muslim who believes in Allah and wishes to be rewarded in heaven to comply with Allah's order to kill the Americans and Jew infidels and plunder their money wherever and whenever they find it. We also call on Muslim leaders, youths, and soldiers to launch raids against Americans and the devil's supporters allying with them, and to displace those who are behind them so that they may learn a lesson.'"

Sharbell put the paper down, then faced the camera again. "Truly an act of desperation, is it not? Is there any way we can avoid this? Is there any way we can make peace with someone whose sole purpose in life now seems to be to kill as many Americans as he can? I think we must find a way, and the one, clear voice of reason in our government now is Harriet Clayton. The wife of the former Vice President, who was perhaps the most active Second Lady in the history of our country, is now the junior Senator from the state of New Jersey. Senator Harriet Clayton will be our guest, and we will talk to her as soon as we come back."

* * *

Dallas:

As the two terrorists moved cautiously down the hallway on the sixty-fifth floor, Linda suddenly stepped out around the corner at the far end of the hall.

"Hey, guys!" she called. "Want some of this?" She pulled the top of her dress down far enough to flash a breast at them.

"Satan's whore!" one of the terrorists shouted. They started running toward her, and Linda darted back around the corner.

As the terrorists rounded the corner, however, they ran straight into John and Don, who were standing there, waiting for them.

"Surprise," John said. He and Don fired a short burst each, and the terrorists went down. John pushed the talk switch on his radio.

"All right, Faysal," he said. "That's two more down. I just thought I would let you know that we're tired of being the hunted. From this point on, we're the hunters."

Back in the ballroom, Faysal looked around. He had only three men remaining with him, and of the three, only one was actually a member of his commando team. The other two, the waiter and the busboy, were sleepers, longtime residents of the United States who had come out from deep cover to kill the First Lady's two Secret Service agents. They were trained as espionage agents, not as warriors, and even now they were armed only with the pistols they had used to kill the Secret Service agents. Faysal had no idea how much help they would be to him in standing off any assault Satan might mount.

In addition to the three men who were with him, Faysal had two more men on the roof. They had been put up there to turn back any attempt to land a SWAT team by helicopter, and they had done their job. Faysal had started this mission with a twelve-man commando squad. He now had only three of his commando squad remaining. Satan had killed all the others.

"Get ready, they are coming!" Faysal said.

The three defenders overturned a table to use as cover, then started watching the door.

From his briefcase, Faysal removed a vest, then put it on. The vest was fully lined with plastique explosive. If Satan and whoever was with him got through, then Faysal's last act would be to detonate the bomb. He would die a martyr's death, be transported instantly to heaven, and would take everyone in this room with him.

He wished the bomb was powerful enough to bring down the entire building the way the airliners crashing into the Twin Towers had brought *them* down. He closed his eyes and imagined the scene. How glorious that would be.

Faysal's reverie was interrupted by the sudden entrance of four people. But it wasn't through the front door as Aziz had expected. Instead, two men and two women came sliding down on ropes, lowered from the overhead skylight.

But what was this? he asked himself. They weren't

wearing the black coveralls of a SWAT team! The men were wearing suits, and the women dresses. Nevertheless, they were carrying weapons and they represented a threat.

"They are here!" Faysal shouted to his three remaining men. But as the men were behind tables, waiting for someone to burst in through the front door, they weren't prepared for an invasion from above.

John shot the one who was dressed as the other terrorists had been dressed, but hesitated when he saw the waiter and the busboy. Were they hostages?

"They're with *them!*" Linda and Jennifer shouted at the same time. They didn't hesitate and were shooting, even as they identified the two planted terrorists.

As Faysal saw his last line of defense go down, he called to the men on the roof. "Hashim, Sharif! The infidels have broken through! Come at once!"

"Allah Akbar!" one of the terrorists replied over the radio. A moment later, those in the ballroom saw a body plummeting down from above.

"He jumped!" someone shouted.

"There's another one!"

Faysal looked around just in time to see the second of the two bodies plunge past the window.

"Looks like that's it, Faysal," John said. "You are all alone now. You may as well give it up."

Faysal began to smile. He put down his gun and raised his hands over his head.

"That's more like it," John said.

Suddenly, Faysal reached inside his vest.

"John! That vest! It's a bomb!" Jennifer shouted. Jennifer was an explosives expert, and it was in that capacity that she was most valuable to the team. If she identified the vest as a bomb, then John wasn't about to question her.

John and Don rushed Faysal. Startled to see them coming toward him, rather than going away, Faysal hesitated just a moment before he activated the detonator. During that moment of hesitation John grabbed Faysal on one side, and Don on the other. Continuing their forward momentum, they picked Faysal up, took three more steps toward the wall, then sent him crashing through the large plate-glass window.

On the street below:

"Here comes another one!" someone shouted, pointing to the third body to come plummeting down in the last few seconds.

As the crowd below watched the body plummet toward the street, they were startled to see it suddenly explode. There was a large flash of fire and a puff of smoke, followed a couple of seconds later by a dull thump. After that, bloody body parts, not one of them bigger than a man's hand, continued the long fall to the ground below.

"Chief Collins, are you there?" a voice asked over the radio.

"Yes, I'm here," Collins said.

"That airburst you just saw was Faysal. It's all clear here now. As soon as we can get the elevators operating again, we'll all come down."

"Good job, Satan," Collins said.

* * *

Washington, D.C., World Satellite News studios:

The set of *Sharbell, the Crying Voice of Reason* was a simple one. It consisted of a small round table, with Sharbell sitting on one side and his guest on the other. Sharbell had emerged onto the public scene during the previous Administration. An apologist for the President, he was rewarded for his service by being given exclusive interviews with high-ranking White House staff members when other reporters were being shut out.

Sharbell called his show *The Crying Voice of Reason*, though conservatives called him The Lying Voice of Treason. Because his liberal credentials were strong, he and the more liberal politicians had a symbiotic relationship going for them. The politicians needed the voice he gave them, and he needed the access they gave him. One of his favorite politicians was, and had been for a long time, Harriet Clayton. During the Administration just passed, Harriet had been a lightning rod, a far more interesting person than the rather mousy First Lady, and thus the subject of intense media scrutiny. The result was a personality that people tended to admire or hate. Few were ambivalent toward her.

Most were surprised when Harriet established a residency in New Jersey, a state in which she had never lived, then announced her intention to run for the Senate. To the shock of nearly everyone, and to the consternation of conservatives everywhere, Harriet won the election.

This was the woman who now sat poised and calm, just across the round table from Douglas Sharbell.

"May I ask you a question?" Sharbell said to Harriet.

Harriet smiled. "Well, of course you can. I mean, after all, isn't that the way this show works? You ask questions of your guests?"

Sharbell chuckled. "Yes, but since most of my guests are politicians, most dissemble when I question them. Very few are candid. One of the reasons I have always appreciated you as a guest is because you have always been honest with the people."

"I have always tried to be," Harriet replied.

"Do you think the President is doing a good job in handling this current crisis?"

"I think we should all get behind our President," Harriet began, but Sharbell held up his hand to stop her.

"No one denies that," he said. "But the question was, do you think the President is doing a good job?"

"I would like to see him be a bit more creative in his approach to foreign policy."

"If you were grading him, what kind of score would you give him?"

"I would give him a C minus."

"That's pretty tough grading."

"We live in tough times."

"If you were President now, would you handle this current crisis differently from the way President Emerson is handling it?"

"Oh, my, if *I* were President?" Harriet replied.

She fanned her face and smiled. "You can turn a girl's head, mentioning me and the Presidency in the same sentence. I didn't expect that question. Most would ask me if my husband had been elected, would he have handled it differently."

"Yes, but your husband wasn't elected and so now it is anyone's ballgame," Sharbell said. "And let's face it, your name is being mentioned in some circles."

"It's much too soon to speculate on any plans I might have along those lines."

"But you won't say here that you have no intention of ever seeking the Presidency?"

"As I said, it is much too soon to speculate on such a thing."

"Very well, but for illustrative purposes only, I will repeat the question. If you were President, would you handle the current crisis any differently?"

Harriet struck a thoughtful pose before she answered, and the camera moved in tight to see the intensity in her clear, blue eyes, the thoughtful expression on a face that was framed by blond hair, which she wore cut short. Her hair hadn't always been short. When she first became Second Lady, she changed her hair so often that there were Web sites established just to keep track of her hairstyles.

"Yes," she finally answered. "Of course I would have handled things differently." She held up her hand. "Now, don't get me wrong, I stand by my earlier statement that we should back the President. After all, we only have one President, and he is doing the best he can. But I think more could be done."

"What more would you do?"

"Well, as you know, Douglas, I once wrote a book called *The World Is My Hometown*. And in that book, I pointed out that with the instantaneous communication, rapid transportation, and economic interdependence of us all, we are truly one little town. The sooner all the world leaders recognize that fact, the sooner we will have a genuine world peace."

"The President has said that he will not meet with Abdul Kadan Kadar because Kadar is a terrorist, and he won't negotiate with terrorists. Do you agree with that policy?"

Harriet shook her head. "I'm afraid I don't agree. What drives Mr. Kadar to such acts of desperation? If we could find what motivates him and others like him to do such, in our eyes, shocking things, perhaps we could find some way to eliminate that motivation. But that can only happen if we are willing to negotiate."

"Would you be willing to talk to Kadar?"

"Yes, of course I would," Harriet replied.

There was a voice in Sharbell's earplug, and he held up his finger as a signal to Harriet to wait a moment. Then he nodded, and turned toward the camera.

"Ladies and gentlemen, we have just been told that the standoff in Dallas is over and that all the hostages have been freed. That includes the First Lady, Mrs. Karen Emerson. We take you now to Dallas."

"And we are clear," the floor director said.

The lights on the set were dimmed, and one of the assistant directors came up to Harriet to remove the little clip-on microphone. Sharbell removed his own lavalier microphone, then stood up.

"Is that it?" Harriet asked. "Is the interview over?"

"I'm afraid it is. They'll be covering the events in Dallas for the rest of the day."

"This was hardly worth coming to the studio for," Harriet said.

"Oh, I don't know about that," Sharbell answered. "I've just floated the first real feeler for you for President."

"You are aware, aren't you, that my husband will probably run again."

"Senator, your husband's political career went down like the *Titanic.* You know it, I know it, and the whole country knows it. If there is ever going to be a Clayton Presidency, it will be Madame President, not Mr. President. And I can help that come about, if you are interested."

"Holy shit! Look at that!" someone said, and everyone looked toward the studio monitor, which was now tuned to the line feed. What they were seeing was Faysal's body plummeting down, then exploding in midair.

"Awesome!" someone in the studio said.

"I can't believe a thoughtful show like this was preempted for the blood and gore they are going to be showing for the rest of the day," Harriet said.

Sharbell held up his hand. "If it was up to me, we would never have cut away," he said. "But it's all a matter of ratings, and even WSN executives know that sensationalism will outdraw thought-provoking programming every time."

"It's the sign of our times," Harriet said. "What did you mean that you could help me become President?"

"Are you interested?"

"I might be."

"Then let me ask you this. Were you serious when you said you would be willing to meet with Abdul Kadan Kadar?"

"You can make that happen?"

Sharbell nodded. "I believe I can," he said.

"All right. Make it happen."

Dallas:

Although Chief Collins and other officials of the Dallas Police, Texas Rangers, and FBI met and debriefed all of the hostages as they left the building, Collins was unable to find the man he had known only as Satan.

"Don't try to find out who he was," Andy Garrison told him when the two men spoke by phone later that afternoon.

"Was he one of your people, Andy?"

"I'm not at liberty to say."

"Well for chrissake, Andy, if you had someone working inside, the least you could have done is let me know. We might have been able to coordinate something. I might not have lost my men when the bomb went off in the stairwell."

"We knew nothing about that," Andy said. "And if it is any consolation to you, I didn't have any control over Satan."

"But you knew he was there?"

"Yes. I knew he was there."

"And you know who he is?"

"Yes."

"But you aren't going to tell me."

"No."

Chief Collins sighed. "Andy, I thought the whole idea of Homeland Security was to coordinate the efforts between all the governmental agencies, federal, state, and local."

"That's true."

"Now you tell me there is some agency out there that nobody knows anything about."

"Let it go, Keith. It worked, didn't it?"

"Yeah, I guess you're right about that. It did work."

"Listen, you and your boys did one hell of a job today. The whole country is proud of you."

"Thanks," Chief Collins said.

Nine

The house sat in an isolated area, far enough from any major road that no one could just happen by. If a car was on the road, it was definitely coming to this house. It was a nice house, the kind of place to which a wealthy CEO might retire. It was stylish and spacious, without being outwardly ostentatious. A casual glance showed how cleverly the architecture managed to blend with the environment, making use as it did of stone and weathered wood. Even the tumbleweed that rolled by added to the intrinsic appeal of the house.

It was not until someone went inside that they could see how unique the house really was. In the room that might be a den in any other house, there was a dazzling array of electronic equipment. There were TV screens, computer terminals, faxes, and copiers. There was also a character- and image-generator that could receive data from a dozen orbiting satellites, then project, onto a wall-sized screen, a detailed picture of just about any place in the world. Further, it could do all this in real time.

Although the Code Team often gathered here for briefings on upcoming operations, or debriefings on operations just completed, it was relatively quiet today, with only John, Don, Jennifer, and Linda here. All other Code Team members were on assignments in various parts of the world. Wagner was here, of course. Wagner lived here and was the liaison between the Code Team and the wealthy men and women whose contributions financed the operations.

John and the others had come straight to the headquarters from Dallas, leaving before any of the other guests could point them out to the media. They had no specific assignment in front of them now, and they planned to use the time here get a little rest and relaxation.

John, Bob Garret, Jennifer, and Linda were sprawled out on leather sofas and chairs in the living room, watching a video on a screen that was nearly as large as the screen in a theater. Bob was wearing shorts, the bandage on his leg still obvious, though not as large as it once was. The video they were watching was an action movie starring Arnold Schwarzenegger.

"If we could get him on our team, he would do all the work and the rest of us could stay home," Bob said.

"Hell, you're staying home now," Jennifer said. "Riding that injury of yours like it was a ticket to a rest home."

"I'm a cripple, have pity on me," Bob said, putting a hand over his wound.

The others laughed.

"But what do you think of my idea of recruiting Schwarzenegger?" Bob asked.

"Schwarzenegger is a wimp," John said.

The others looked at John in surprise.

"Whoa, hold it, you're calling Arnold Schwarzengger a wimp?" Linda asked.

"So, who do you like? Sylvester Stallone? Jean-Claude Van Damme?" Jennifer asked.

"Nope. The one we should get is Clint Eastwood."

"Clint Eastwood? Are you serious?"

"Yes, I'm serious. You ever see any of Clint Eastwood's movies? He doesn't mess around with people. If they need to be shot, ole Clint just shoots them." Then, in his best Clint Eastwood impersonation, John said, "Well, do ya, punk? Come on, make my day."

Bob and the women were laughing as Wagner came through the living room, carrying a tray on which there was piled a prodigious amount of food.

"Wagner, good man," Bob said, reaching for the tray. "I was getting a little hungry."

"Sorry, this isn't for you folks," Wagner said. "It's for Don."

"All of that is for Don?" Jennifer asked.

"You know how much he eats," Linda said.

"Yes, but I didn't think even Don would eat that much."

"Well, you have to understand that he is working hard right now," Wagner said. "And hard work brings out an appetite."

"How's he doing in there?" John asked.

"Why don't you go to one of the business channels and see for yourself?" Wagner asked.

"Business channels?" Bob asked.

Picking up the remote, John clicked off the movie, then clicked on one of the business channels. There were two analysts sitting behind a desk. Chroma-keyed behind them was a large chart.

". . . amazing comeback," the announcer was saying. "As expected, this morning when the stock market opened for the first time since the terrorists attacks over the weekend, it took a monstrous hit. The Dow fell so far that we fully expected the circuit breakers to automatically halt trading, but just before that happened, bargain hunters moved in."

"Yes, Lou, and some of the bargain hunters aren't merely playing with the market, they are moving the market. There have been several purchases worth one hundred million dollars."

"Do we know who they are?" Lou asked.

"Amazingly, we do not," the analyst replied. "And that is unusual because there aren't that many people in the country, or the world for that matter, who can make such purchases. And yet, it doesn't seem to be any of them."

"This is a real mystery then," Lou replied. "It would appear that we may have another Warren Buffett figure, someone who has made a fortune from the stock market but has, thus far, managed to keep his, or her, identity secret."

"Whoever it is, the nation's economy has him to thank. Because of these massive purchases, it now appears as if the stock market will not suffer from this latest series of events, and indeed, might even prosper."

Watching the two men discuss in wonder what

was going on with the stock market, John shook his head and chuckled. "Don, do your thing," he said under his breath. He walked into the computer room to see what was going on.

Don was sitting cross-legged on a chair in front of a computer monitor. For the moment he was just watching the screen and eating a sandwich that was so big it took both hands to handle it.

"Don?" John called.

"Wait," Don said, holding up a finger. He stared at the screen for a moment longer, then hit the enter key. When he looked up at John, his smile was as broad as his face. "All finished," he said.

"What did you do?"

"Well, all day today I've been doing some bodacious day trading. Now I've constructed a path for all the money to return to the original accounts, except for Kadar's money. I figure that by noon tomorrow, all the money will be back in its rightful place."

"Why so long? Why not put it all back now?"

"It's too much money for a vertical move," Don said. "It had to be dragged through the market in order to keep down the spikes."

"Well, answer me this, Mr. Yee. Did we profit from all this manipulation?" John asked.

"Come look," Don said.

John stepped around behind Don, then looked at a small information box in the lower right corner of the screen. "Can you see the figure in that box?" Don teased. "Or are you such an old man that you need glasses?"

"I can see it," John said. He read the number

aloud. "Twenty-seven million, six hundred thousand, four hundred and twelve."

"That is how much we enriched our account," Don said.

"Damn, Don, if crooks could manipulate the system the way you do, there would never be another armed robbery."

"Yeah," Don said, and the smile left his face. "And when they learn that, it's going to be disastrous for us all."

Washington, D.C., Oval Office, next day:

"Wait a minute," President Emerson said into the phone. "Are you telling me that all the money the terrorists extorted from Bates and the others has been returned?"

"Yes, sir, that's what I'm telling you," Jason Carter replied. Jason Carter was deputy director of the Securities and Exchange Commission. "The money has not only been returned, but with five-percent interest earned over the seventy-two hours it was gone."

"But who returned it?"

"Uh, that we don't know, sir."

"Do you know where it has been?"

"No, sir, we don't know that either, though we suspect that it was the engine used to keep the stock market from collapsing after this weekend."

"Well, I don't know who did it, or how they did it, but the nation owes them a debt of gratitude," President Emerson said.

"Mr. President, I don't think I would make any public announcements about this if I were you," Carter said.

"Why is that?"

"Because whoever it is violated at least a dozen or more SEC regulations, federal laws, and may have even committed larceny on a grand scale."

"But he saved the nation's economy," Emerson said.

"Yes, sir, I'll grant you that," Carter answered. "But he did it with the unauthorized use of a tremendous amount of money for seventy-two hours. That's grand larceny, and combined with all the other laws that were broken, he, or she, might be looking at forty years in prison."

"Not while I'm President. I'm going to issue a full pardon."

"That might not be a good idea, Mr. President," Carter said. "At this point I think it might be best just to step away from the whole thing."

"By 'step away from the whole thing,' are you saying that the SEC is going to let it go as well?"

"Yes, sir. Unless we get a specific complaint from someone, we aren't going to investigate."

"That's good. I'm glad to see that somewhere under all the bureaucratic red tape, there is a modicum of common sense."

Carter chuckled. "We aren't all products of the Government Printing Office," he said.

"You're doing a good job over there, Jason. Let me know if any of this threatens to get out of hand."

"I will, sir."

* * *

In the sky over Sitarkistan, 0300:

Three B-52's, each carrying twenty two-thousand-pound bombs, flew through the darkness over the southern range of the Sitarkistan Mountains. The mountains housed a network of interconnected caves known to be bases for members of the Islamic Jihad Muhahidin.

"Arc Light One, this is Compass Call," a radar controller on board an orbiting AWAC called.

"Arc Light One, go," the pilot of the lead B-52 responded.

"Turn now to a heading of zero-six-zero degrees."

"Roger, zero-six-zero."

The three bombers moved in concert, turning to the new course.

"Countdown begins now," the AWAC controller said. "Bomb release in four-five seconds."

"Bomb bay doors open," the pilot commanded.

There was an electronic whir that couldn't be heard directly by the B-52 crew, though they could hear a whine through the earphones of their flight helmets. The pilot could feel the increased drag on the airplane as the huge doors swung open.

"Bomb release in two-zero seconds," the AWAC controller said.

"Bombs armed," the bombardier called.

"Zero-five seconds."

The bombardier studied his panel, watching the seconds tick down. As the counter turned to zero-zero, a series of red lights began flashing, indicating that the bombs were being automatically released. A clean board told him that all bombs were gone.

"All bombs away," he said matter-of-factly.

"Arc Light Two, Arc Light Three, report status," the pilot of Arc Light One called.

"Arc Light Two, all bombs away."

"Arc Light Three, all bombs away."

"Compass Call, all bombs away," Arc Light One called.

"Very good, sir. Turn now to course two-seven-zero for target departure."

"Two-seven-zero."

The three bombers made the turn while, five miles below them, 120 thousand pounds of bombs had another two miles to fall before impact.

Omar Jumah sat on a rock in front of a cave, smoking a cigarette and fantasizing about the glory of battle. Lovingly, he stroked the AK-47 he was carrying and pictured himself killing Americans. He hated Americans, he hated the way they were so contemptuous of all things pure and holy, and the way they let their women parade around nearly naked.

He saw an American magazine once—he couldn't remember the name of it, but it had many pictures of naked American women. They were young, and beautiful, and naked. They were an abomination, whores of Satan for allowing themselves to be photographed in such a way.

And yet now, even as he recalled the pictures, he could feel himself getting an erection. He wished he had an American woman here, right now. He would throw her down in the dirt and use her, show her his contempt for her.

When he heard the whistling sounds from above, he had no idea what it was, for he had never been under aerial bombardment before. But even though he didn't know what it was, he felt his body being taken over by a cold terror. He had only seconds of terror before the world exploded around him, and Omar Jumah ceased to exist.

Within twelve hours, headlines around the world reported on America's retaliatory raid against suspected hideouts of the Islamic Jihad Muhahidin.

MANY KILLED IN U.S. BOMBING RAID
ONE VILLAGE REDUCED TO RUBBLE
WOMEN AND CHILDREN AMONG THE
VICTIMS OF U.S. BOMBS
ARAB NATIONS CALL FOR A HALT
IN BOMBING

World Satellite Network Studios:

"My guest tonight, on *The Crying Voice of Reason,* is Prince Rahman Rashid Yazid," Sharbell said as he introduced his show. "Prince Rahman is a member of the ruling family of Sitarkistan, a general in the Sitarkistan Air Force, and director of Children's Relief Fund of Sitarkistan. Prince Rahman, thank you for appearing tonight."

"Thank you for having me on," Yazid replied on the satellite feed from Sitarkistan.

"The entire world wants to know, Prince Rahman, if the American government contacted your government prior to the bombing attacks on your country."

"They did not," Yazid replied. "But they have since requested permission to use one of our airfields as a base of their operations."

"Is your government going to allow that?"

"We will have to discuss it. As you know, our two nations have enjoyed a long friendship, and we wish to see this relationship continue. We deplore the terrorists' attacks against America, and are embarrassed that the man who orchestrated the attacks was born in and resides in Sitarkistan. I hasten to point out, however, that his citizenship has been revoked."

"Even though your government wasn't contacted prior to the bombing attack, do you approve of the attack?"

"We approve of it in principle," Yazid said. "However, had we known in advance, we could have perhaps spared the lives of the innocent women and children who lived in the small village of Hindakar. The bombs fell on them, as well as the camp of the Islamic Jihad Muhahidin. But tragically, the bombs weren't the only means by which our country was attacked."

"What do you mean when you say the bombing wasn't the only way your country was attacked? The U.S. attacked in some other way?"

"No, the attack I'm talking about was not, I believe, a U.S. Government operation. Rather, it was the work of terrorism against Islam."

"Anti-Islamic terrorists?"

"Yes, and the attack launched against us was much more cowardly than the attack launched against America. In the attack on America, what the U.S. Government is calling a terrorist attack, brave men martyred themselves for a cause they believed in. But the attack against my country was launched by a coward, hiding in a darkened room somewhere while sitting in front of a computer."

"I will get to that in a moment, Prince, but first I must address something you just said. You said America was attacked by brave men. I'm afraid that most Americans don't see it that way. They look at what happened as despicable acts, perpetrated by fanatics."

"Yes, yes," Yazid said dismissively. "Don't get me wrong, I am not supporting what happened, merely stating the fact that they were men of courage who gave their lives for a cause in which they believed. And whether you agree with their objectives or not, I'm sure you will understand that, in Muslim countries, these men will be honored for their courage and sacrifice."

"One of those men was a lieutenant in your Air Force, I believe," Sharbell pointed out.

"That claim has been made, yes," Yazid said.

"That claim? Are you saying that you don't believe it?"

"I am merely saying that I wish to withhold judgment until there is positive identification of the remains."

"All right, I can see that. Now, about the attack you call a terrorist attack against your country, what was it, and how did it take place?"

"A computer hacker—we believe it to be an American hacker—broke into the account of the Children's Relief Fund of Sitarkistan and stole millions of dollars."

"Wait a minute, you're not talking about some hacker who breaks in and leaves a virus of some sort . . . a practical joker. You're saying that whoever hacked into that account stole money?" Sharbell asked.

"A great deal of money, yes. Money that was to have been used to feed our children, clothe them, and provide medical assistance for them. That ability has been taken from us, at the very moment we need it most, to assist the children who were orphaned by American bombing of the village of Hindakar."

"Do you have any idea who might have done such a thing?"

"We don't know exactly who it was," Yazid answered. "But we did trace the funds into the American stock market. After that, we lost track of it. The stock market was so volatile over the last two days that it became impossible to follow what was going on."

"I understand you have filed a complaint with the American Government, and with the Securities and Exchange Commission," Sharbell said.

"We have, though what good will come of the complaint, we don't know."

Code Name headquarters:

"I'll be damned," Don said as he was watching TV. "If the money was taken from the Sitarkistan

Children's Relief Fund account, then that means the Children's Relief Fund is a front for the Islamic Jihad Muhahidin."

"You're sure?" Linda asked.

"Of course I'm sure. When I hacked in, I just followed the money to its source, then constructed a bridge that transferred it to our account."

"Is there any way they can trace where it went?" John asked.

Don shook his head. "No way," he said. "I put up a firewall to block it."

"If Prince Rahman Rashid Yazid represents this Children's Relief Fund, then he must be affiliated with the Islamic Jihad Muhahidin," Linda suggested.

"Yeah, well, I don't know why that should surprise anyone," John said. "After the Trade Center bombings, wasn't it proven that Osama Bin Laden was getting a substantial part of his funding from so-called charitable operations?"

"Yes, it was. And I'm not surprised to see part of Sitarkistan's Royal Family involved either," Jennifer said.

"What amazes me is that he has the audacity to make the claim that someone took money from that account. Isn't that just admitting that it is the terrorists' account?" Linda asked.

Don shook his head. "Not necessarily," he said. "Nobody but us can make the connection between that account and the terrorists."

"And we can't say anything without compromising our position," John said.

"Yes, well, it blisters my ass that the son of a bitch

is on television now, crying like he is the victim," Jennifer said.

John laughed. "And that's a shame, because your ass is much too cute to be blistered."

"If I were you, mister, I'd worry less about my ass and more about your balls, because any more sexist remarks like that and I'm going to hand them to you."

"Holy shit, John, I think she means it," Don said. Then all four laughed.

Ten

Former Vice President Eddie Clayton and Senator Harriet Clayton owned two houses, one in Georgetown, and one in Newark, New Jersey. In addition, they kept an apartment on Central Park West in New York because Eddie Clayton had an office in Manhattan. Ostensibly, the former Vice President was a political consultant, and he commanded rather large fees for showing up at political fund-raising events. The office also served as the headquarters for his Presidential campaign, though as he had not yet officially announced, his candidacy was behind the scenes.

Harriet rarely made an appearance at the Manhattan apartment. In fact she had only a few changes of clothes there, and probably had not spent more than five or six nights in residence. Eddie, on the other hand, stayed at the apartment more than he did at both other houses combined.

The doorman was surprised to see Harriet breeze by when she arrived unexpectedly on Wednesday afternoon. He was so surprised that for a full moment after she started up to the seventeenth floor, he continued to sit there, staring at the elevator doors. Then, suddenly, he realized what he must do, and he picked up the phone and dialed.

Ginger Alexander looked sweet and innocent, but it became obvious, soon after she came to work in Eddie Clayton's office, that she wasn't innocent. She was overtly sexual around him, letting him know in every way that she was available. One day she came into his office wearing a ridiculously short skirt and no panties. Conveniently dropping something on the floor in front of his desk, she bent over to pick it up, making certain that he got an eyeful.

While still bent over, Ginger looked around at Eddie to check his reaction.

"Do you like what you see?" she asked.

"Who wouldn't?" Eddie answered.

Straightening up, Ginger smiled. "Well, I like to please. Oh, can I ask your opinion on something?"

"Sure."

Ginger pulled up her skirt. "As you can see, I've shaved my pubes. Do you think it makes me look too young?"

"How, uh, how old are you, honey?" Eddie asked. His tongue was thick and his breathing shallow.

"I'm nineteen, but everyone says that I don't look any older than fifteen. I guess shaving my pubes makes it even worse, huh?"

"Worse? No, that's not a term I would use," Eddie said. "I think it, uh, you—are very attractive."

"Do you find me desirable?"

"Desirable? Yes, of course."

"Desirable enough for you to have sex with me?"

Eddie cleared his throat. "Let me get this straight. Are you *asking* me to have sex with you?"

"Yes," Ginger said. "I mean, you can do it, can't you? Everything works?"

Eddie laughed. "Yes, everything works. Sometimes I wish it didn't."

"So, do you want to have sex with me?"

"Honey, are you sure you know what you are getting into?" Eddie asked her. "You have to understand that there's no future in it for you."

"I'm not looking for a future, I'm looking for excitement," Ginger said. "And I can't think of anything more exciting than doing the Vice President of the United States. Except maybe the President."

"I'm not the Vice President anymore."

"No, but you were. And one day you're going to be President."

"From your mouth to God's ear," Eddie said.

Saying that he had a meeting to attend, Eddie left the office with Ginger, and they went Eddie's apartment on Central Park West. Ginger proved to be quite inventive, and for a while Eddie could almost believe that there was no world beyond this apartment, this bedroom, this bed. He was riding a rocket, he was soaring through the stars, he was . . . hearing bells. Damn it! He really *was* hearing bells. The phone was ringing.

At first he tried to ignore it, but he couldn't. The ringing was spoiling the mood, taking away everything. With a sigh of frustration, he grabbed the phone.

"What?" he shouted in anger.

"Mr. Vice President, this is Angelo, the doorman. I thought you ought to know that Senator Clayton is on her way up."

"What? Shit!" Eddie said. He sighed. "Thanks, Angelo."

"Yes, sir."

Sitting up on the edge of the bed, Eddie pulled on his trousers, not bothering to put on his underwear. He pushed his underwear under the bed. "Get dressed," he said.

"What is it?" Ginger asked.

"My wife is on her way up."

"Your wife? I thought she never came to this apartment."

"She comes only rarely. This is one of those rare times."

From the front room, Eddie could hear the key in the latch. Then the door opened, but it was caught by the chain guard.

"What the hell? Eddie! Open the door!" Harriet called.

"What should I do?" Ginger asked, sitting on the edge of the bed and covering her small but well-formed breasts with one arm.

"Hell, honey, you don't have to cover up for me," Eddie said. "I've seen everything you have. But I would suggest that you get dressed." He pulled on a pullover shirt, then walked out into the front room. Taking the remote from the coffee table, he clicked on the TV as he headed toward the door.

"I didn't expect you," Eddie said as he released the chain. "You should've called."

"You mean, make an appointment?"

"No, nothing like that. I mean, I wasn't doing anything but watching TV."

Glancing toward the TV, Harriet chuckled. "An infomercial? Anyway, I didn't know until the last minute that I was going to be able to get away," Harriet said.

"Are you just stopping by?"

"No, I'm going to stay a few days," Harriet said. "I've got some morning TV shows I'll be doing. After my appearance with Sharbell, several of the shows have contacted me."

"Yes, I saw you on Sharbell's show."

"What did you think?"

"What do I think?" Eddie repeated. "I think it sounds like you are getting ready to launch your own campaign for President, that's what I think."

"I didn't say that."

"No, you didn't say that. But when you had the opportunity to put it aside, once and for all, you didn't. 'It's much too soon to speculate on any plans I might have along those lines,' you said."

"What did you expect me to say? That is the standard answer of just about any politician in America, you know that."

"Yes, but not a politician whose husband just missed the Presidency by a fraction of a percentage point, and who is already engaged in the next Presidential campaign."

"You're being paranoid," Harriet said. "And I

don't have time to deal with your paranoia now."
She started toward the bedroom.

"Where are you going?"

"To change clothes," Harriet said. "I know I have
a pair of sweats here."

"Wait, I'll get them for you."

Harriet laughed. "So I can do what? Change in
the living room and watch the infomercial?" She
was still laughing when she opened the door to the
bedroom, but the laugh turned to a gasp when she
saw Ginger in her panties and bra, reaching for her
dress.

"Who are you?" Harriet asked coldly.

"Ginger Alexander," Ginger answered in a
frightened voice. "I, uh, work for your husband.
I was just, uh . . ." She was unable to finish her
sentence.

"Yes, I know what you were doing," Harriet said.
She looked at the young, half-naked girl, then at
the mussed bed.

Eddie came to the open door. "Harriet, I know
what you are thinking," he said.

Harriet shook her head. "No, you don't have the
slightest idea of what I'm thinking."

"Sure I do. You're thinking that I promised you
nothing like this would happen again, but damn it
what do you expect from me? You are never here,
and a man has needs."

"Oh, bullshit, Eddie, cut the crap," Harriet said.
"I've never been able to satisfy your needs, nor do I
have any desire or intention to even try. What I'm
thinking is, if you are so damned awkward that your
own wife can catch you in flagrante delicto, do you

think for one minute that reporters won't?" She waved her hand in disgust.

"Senator Clayton, please don't blame the Vice President. It is really my fault," Ginger said. "I came on to him and . . ."

"Honey, disabuse yourself of any idea that you caused this by offering him your ass. As cute as your little ass is, it has nothing to do with it. Eddie Clayton would fuck a bush if he thought there was a snake in it. Now, get your things and get out of here. Oh, and whatever work you were doing for my husband? Forget about it. You're fired."

"Yes, ma'am," Ginger said, breaking into tears.

"You can't fire her, she doesn't work for you," Eddie said.

"Very well then. You fire her."

Eddie stared hard at Harriet for a long moment, then sighed and looked at Ginger. "You're fired," he said.

Zebakabad, Sitarkistan:

Prince Rahman Rashid Yazid was holding the weekly Session of Appeals, so called because, once a week, a member of the Royal Family would meet with subjects of Sitarkistan to hear their appeals and grievances. The Session of Appeals operated on a first-come, first-served basis, and those who sought a royal audience came from all walks of life, from oil-rich businessmen looking for a favorable ruling on a multimillion-dollar deal, to the lowest street beggar, wanting enough money for his next meal.

Most came to ask for royal intercession in some dispute, but many came bearing gifts. It was, the Yazid family pointed out, a perfect example of why a benevolent monarchy was far superior to any democratic government. "Can you imagine," they liked to say, "the President of the United States meeting face-to-face with a street person from Detroit?"

Prince Rahman picked up his porcelain teacup, which was cobalt blue, trimmed in real gold. The cup alone was worth more than the combined yearly income of half the people who were now standing in line. He took a sip of tea as he listened to the plea of the man standing before him now.

The man's name was Malik El Salim, and he was a mid-level bureaucrat in the Sitarkistan Government. He had just asked for intercession on behalf of his daughter. The woman had been sentenced to die by stoning because of an act of adultery. Her adulterous partner was one of Prince Rahman's own brothers. In fact, he himself had once had sex with the woman.

"I beg of you, oh, Noble One, to please spare the life of my daughter," the father said.

Prince Rahman pinched the bridge of his nose. This was one of those moments that would call upon all the skills and leadership qualities a ruler could muster. Because of his and his brother's involvement with the woman, it would be so easy to pardon her. But would it be right? He shook his head. He could not pardon her.

"I'm sorry, Malik, but I cannot grant your daughter a pardon. She has sinned against Allah, and were I to pardon her, her sin would be mine as well."

The expression in Malik's eyes was one of despair. He had already lost his case in the court of appeals, and royal intercession was his last hope.

"However, I will order that she be beheaded, rather than stoned," Prince Rahman offered. "In that way her death will be quick and painless."

"You are most kind," Malik said, putting his hands together and bowing before he left.

As Malik walked away, Prince Rahman took another swallow of his tea. He was glad he was able to come up with a sensible compromise. It was, he was sure, another example of the extraordinary skills Allah bestowed upon the ruling family. No ordinary person would have been able to find a solution to the dilemma that had confronted him.

"Your Excellency, I have a gift for you from one who sends his love and admiration."

Bowing his head, the man approached the throne. He held out a small jade tiger.

Prince Rahman took the tiger.

"Thank you," he said.

The man bowed, then left.

Prince Rahman stood up. "This week's session is over," he announced to those who were still waiting for him. One man, who was legless, had been waiting for six hours, laboriously moving himself through the line by gnarled and calloused knuckles. He would have been next, and he looked entreatingly at Prince Rahman, who turned to one of his attendants.

"Give this man one hundred sitarks," he said, nodding toward the legless one. One hundred sitarks was equal to ten U.S. dollars.

Prince Rahman left the Chamber of the People,

and went to a small room in the rear of the palace. When he opened the door to the little room, he saw a man standing at the rear of the room, looking through the window.

"You sent me the tiger, Abdul?" Prince Rahman said. The jade tiger was a signal that Abdul Kadan Kadar wanted to meet with him.

Kadar turned away from the window.

"You have not put money back into the account," Kadar said accusingly.

"No, I have not."

"I thought you were going to."

"I will, trust me, I will," Prince Rahman replied.

"When?"

"When I think it is safe. You asked for five million dollars. That is a lot of money."

"You have billions of dollars," Kadar said.

Prince Rahman shook his head. "No. The family has billions of dollars. I do not."

"But you have access to it."

"I cannot access that much money without arousing suspicion. I must find some way to move it," Prince Rahman said.

"We are broke, do you understand?" Kadar said. "I cannot pay my men. I cannot carry on the holy battle against the infidels if I have no money. I cannot even feed the men who are with me."

"I can give you one hundred thousand dollars now, today," Prince Rahman said.

Kadar spit on the floor. "One hundred thousand dollars? That is nothing."

"It will feed you until I can find a way to transfer the rest of the money."

"When the revolution comes, and it will come," Kadar said, holding up his finger, "your only hope of remaining in power will be by my good graces."

"Do not threaten me with such talk," Prince Rahman said. "Do you know how easily I could have the Islamic Jihad Muhahidin crushed? The Americans would be most generous to me for the information I could provide them."

Kadar backed away from his rhetoric. "Of course you could, Your Excellency," he said. "I know that you are supporting us because of your faith, and your love for Allah. I did not mean what I said as a threat, but as a guarantee that your position will always be secure."

"Yes, thank you," Prince Rahman said. "I will do what I can to get more money to you."

"Some day, perhaps we will find out what happened to our money," Kadar said. "With my own eyes, I watched it happen on the monitor. One moment we had nearly one billion dollars in our account, and the next moment all the money was gone. If I find who did it, he will pray to Allah that his mother be cast into hell for the sin of giving him birth."

Eleven

Henry Norton, Senator Harriet Clayton's Administrative Assistant, was going through a pile of communication memos on his desk. When he saw one from Douglas Sharbell, he picked up the phone to return the call.

"Doug, this is Henry Norton, Senator Clayton's AA."

"I prefer to be called Douglas."

"Douglas, yes," Henry said. "I'm returning your call."

"I didn't call you, I called the Senator."

"She's not in this afternoon. Could I take a message?"

"I tell you what, Billy boy," Douglas said. "I know you can get hold of her by cell phone, pager, or something. So you get hold of her and you tell her to call me back within thirty minutes."

"Can I tell her what it is about?"

"Thirty minutes," Douglas said. "And the clock is ticking. If she doesn't call within thirty minutes, don't bother."

"I'll, uh, see what I can do," Henry said. He hung

up the phone, then stared at it for a moment. "Asshole," he said.

Less that four minutes after Douglas hung up, his phone rang.

"Good, he got hold of you, I see," Douglas said by way of answering the phone. "I was confident that he would."

"Your confidence borders on arrogance," Harriet said. "What do you want?"

"Were you serious when you said you would like to meet with Abdul Kadan Kadar? Or were you just blowing smoke?"

"Yes, I was serious."

"How serious?"

"Why are you asking? Are you suggesting you can set up such a meeting?"

"Maybe."

"That's impossible," Harriet said. "Right now the government has a twenty-million-dollar reward out for Kadar. The Air Force is making little rocks out of big rocks, trying to get to him with their bombs, and the CIA has been looking for him since the attack began. What makes you think you can find him?"

"Because I have something Kadar wants," Douglas said. "I have a television show that will allow him to present his agenda to the entire world."

"Have you talked to him?" Harriet asked, clearly interested.

"I have talked to someone who has talked to him. And who can talk to him again. But I hope you understand, this is risky business. I don't want to go any further with this unless you are serious about it."

"I am very serious about it," Harriet insisted.

"You know, since Abdul Kadan Kadar has been placed on the most-wanted list, any association with him would be a violation of U.S. law," Douglas warned.

"I think we could get around that," Harriet replied. "If you can get to this man, if you can arrange a meeting between him and me, then let's do it."

"You understand also that I reserve the right to be present at that meeting, and to videotape it for my audience?" Douglas asked.

"I understand."

"Actually, the exposure will be great for your political future," Douglas said.

"I'm doing this for the nation, not for my political career. I was just elected to the Senate. I have a while to go before I have to start worrying about reelection."

"I wasn't talking about reelection to the Senate," Douglas said. "I was talking about your run for the Presidency."

"I've told you, running for President is my husband's game, not mine."

"Senator, if we're going to work together, there's one thing you've got to learn," Douglas said.

"And what is that?"

"Never bullshit a bullshitter. You and I both know that your husband's political future is toast. You, on the other hand, have a clean slate, and the entire world before you."

"Yes, well, we'll see," Harriet said. "In the meantime, do what you can to set up the meeting."

"I'll get right on it."

Zebakabad, Sitarkistan:

Omar Muhammad Yazid, King of Sitarkistan, lit an American cigarette, inhaled, then blew out a long cloud of blue smoke to hover over the meeting table. He had called this meeting of the Council of Princes to discuss the latest request made by the U.S. Government.

"They want to station their warplanes at our airport?" Rahman asked. "Never!"

"We have no choice," Kamali Nuri Yazid said. "Right now they are conducting unrestricted bombing raids in the south of our country. If we do not cooperate with them, it will give the illusion that we are unable to defend ourselves from attack. We will lose face with our allies, our enemies, and even with our own people. We must maintain the façade of a strong personal friendship and alliance with the United States."

"I would think it is the other way around," Rahman said. "Everyone knows that oil rules the world. We have oil, they need oil. They will do whatever we want."

King Omar spoke then. "I would remind my son that while they need our oil, we need their money. We also need their technological support in getting the oil out. Kamali is correct. To the rest of the world, it must look as if we are partners with the United States in their war against Abdul Kadan Kadar."

"Father, Kadar is one of our own people. He is even one of our family, he is a cousin."

"He is the nephew of your mother, Rahman, he

is not *my* nephew," King Yazid reminded him. "And he is unstable. I think we may be better off without him."

"How will it look to our people if we let the Americans in here? Do you think they will approve?"

"Our people approve of the life we have given them," King Omar said. "And that life is made possible by our cooperation with the Americans. I will grant them use of our airport." As King Omar's statement was preemptive, the discussion was over. Like it or not, the Americans would be coming to Sitarkistan.

Leaving the conference, Prince Rahman drove around the city in his Mercedes. He picked up his satellite phone and called a number in Washington, D.C.

Washington, D.C.:

"I'm glad you called," Douglas said. "Are you going to be able to set up a meeting for us?"

"Yes," Prince Rahman replied. "But you must tell no one you are coming."

"Don't worry about that," Douglas said. "I've been in this business for a long time and I've gone underground for sources before."

"And the Senator? She understands the rules?"

"I will make certain she understands the rules," Douglas said. "How soon can you set the meeting up?"

"How soon can you get here?"

"It may take me a few days to get things arranged here," Douglas said. "Say, one week?"

"I will send you instructions on where to come," Prince Rahman said.

The Saudi-Sitarkistan border, one week later:

Three of them made the trip from the United States: Harriet, Douglas, and Douglas's cameraman, George Murdock. Harriet wanted her Administrative Assistant to come as well, but Douglas told her that the rules set down for the meeting were very strict. They either followed the rules as established, or there would be no meeting. Reluctantly, Harriet agreed to leave her AA behind.

The three of them were met in Peshawar, Pakistan, by a bearded man Harriet thought was a skycap. Instead, the man informed them that he was the pilot who would be taking them on the next leg of their journey.

"And just where would that be?" Douglas asked.

"You will see," the pilot answered as he picked up one suitcase, leaving the other for Douglas to carry. When the cameraman started with them, the pilot stopped and held up his hand. "You cannot come," he said.

"What? What do you mean he can't come? He is my cameraman."

"Only two can come," the pilot said.

"I protest this. It was agreed that I could tape this for broadcast. How can I do that without my cameraman?"

"Only two can come," the pilot repeated.

Harriet laughed.

"What's so funny?"

"You didn't have any trouble telling me that my AA would have to stay behind. Rules aren't as much fun when they hit *you*, are they?"

Douglas ran his hand through his hair, then sighed in frustration. He reached for the camera. "All right, George, wait here for us," he said. "I'll figure out some way to handle it. Come on, let's go."

Walking briskly across the tarmac, they followed the pilot toward a small, high-winged airplane. The airplane was sitting among other small planes, on the opposite side of the terminal from the larger commercial aircraft.

"Will someone meet us when we land?" Harriet asked.

"Yes," the pilot replied tersely.

The pilot put the bags behind the rear seat, then held out his hand indicating that Harriet should crawl into the back, while Douglas would take the right front seat.

"Why does he get the front seat?" Harriet asked.

"He is heaviest," the pilot answered without going into an explanation of the dynamics of weight and balance in a small plane.

The pilot climbed into the left front seat and, after flipping a few switches and moving a few levers, started the engine. It kicked off, not with a deep-throated and reassuring roar, but with an irritating buzz that was not much more substantial than the popping sound made by a chain saw.

"Who will meet us?" Douglas asked.

"Someone," the pilot said as the plane started forward.

Although Harriet and Douglas were asking questions, they really didn't expect much more in the way of answers than they received. It had been like this from the moment Abdul Kadan Kadar had agreed to meet with them.

Harriet had not left an itinerary with her office because she had no idea where she would be. At every step along the way they were given instructions only for the very next segment of the trip. They left Dulles International, not knowing what country would be their final destination. So far, they had been in Rome, Istanbul, Cairo, Tehran, Islamabad, and Peshawar. At each stop they were met as soon as they deplaned. Some of their escorts were men and some were women. None seemed to be of any identifiable ethnic heritage. These contacts would provide tickets and instructions for the next destination. As the two departed Peshawar, however, there was a change in the procedure. This was the first time they had traveled on anything other than a commercial airliner. That gave rise to the hope that the journey was almost over.

Harriet Clayton sat gripping the seat with both hands as the airplane pitched and yawed through the roiling air, and at this particular moment she was afraid that the journey might be over even sooner than she wanted.

The pilot seemed dedicated to the proposition of killing them all. They were, right now, flying through a mountain pass. Harriet closed her eyes as the airplane lurched wildly. She felt the plane bank violently as the pilot just managed to avoid crashing into the side of a mountain.

"Must we fly *through* the pass?" Harriet asked in a shaky voice. "Can't we go *over?*" She demonstrated with her hands.

"Radar," was the pilot's one-word answer.

Harriet knew nothing about airplanes. She didn't know if the pilot meant they were trying to avoid radar, or if he was using radar to navigate, or if perhaps he didn't have radar and needed it to fly over the pass. The answer made absolutely no sense to her, so she just closed her eyes and said a prayer as they wallowed on through the turbulent sky.

A few minutes later the wild gyrations stopped, the flight leveled out, and Harriet felt them beginning a descent. When she opened her eyes, she saw a tiny village in front of them.

"Where are we?"

"Khurashar."

There was no airport in Khurashar, but there was a dirt landing strip just northeast of the village. The pilot put the airplane down smoothly, then taxied to the far end of the strip. A jeep was driving out to meet them, marking its transit with the rooster tail of dust that billowed up behind it.

The pilot killed the engine and Douglas and Harriet, both a little shaky from the flight, got out. They stood alongside the plane, listening to the descending hum of the instrument gyros and the snapping and popping of the cooling engine. Standing there for a moment, Harriet breathed in the fresh air, enjoying the feel of solid ground beneath her feet, though she wasn't entirely sure her knees would continue to support her.

Like the pilot, the jeep driver was wearing a turban and full beard. Unlike the pilot, however, the driver was armed, carrying an AK-47. Without comment, he slung his weapon over his shoulder, then took Harriet's luggage from the pilot and carried both bags over to the jeep.

No one gave them an airline ticket, nor were they taken to another private airplane. Because of that, and the fact that this was the first armed contact they had encountered, Harriet was absolutely positive that their destination lay no farther away than the other end of this jeep ride. She hoped it was a short one.

As they drove away from the tiny village, Harriet looked at the towering and rugged Sitarkistan Mountains. She was a long way from downstate Illinois, where she had grown up. Winning a scholarship to Harvard University, she'd met Edward Clayton. Both were politically active in college, and they developed a friendship and working relationship that eventually led to marriage.

They continued their political activism after graduating from college, and with her help, Eddie Clayton was elected governor of South Carolina. After two terms as governor, he was elected Vice President of the United States. It was then that Harriet burst upon the national scene.

She was a Senator now, and though she had denied it, both to Douglas and to her husband, the goal of becoming the first woman President no longer seemed that far out of reach. But to accomplish that goal, she was going to have to take risks, both political and physical. And meeting with Abdul Kadan Kadar was a risk on both levels.

Kadar agreed to meet with her, provided their meeting be kept secret from everyone until after she had returned. Harriet agreed to the terms, swearing her AA to secrecy, and not even telling her husband what she had in mind. Kadar had gone to great lengths to keep the meeting a secret, and Harriet was convinced that not even those people she had met at the various stops along the way knew anything beyond their own little piece of information. It wasn't that they were being uncommunicative when she asked them questions. It was just that they didn't know the answers.

Harriet remembered reading about the French Underground. It seemed that they had worked in the same disconnected way during World War II. There were cells that would transport downed allied pilots back to safety, never knowing where the pilots came from, nor where they would go after they left. It didn't take much for Harriet to imagine that she was like one of those downed pilots now.

Despite the inconvenience and discomfort she had experienced during this trip, and the gravity of the mission, Harriet felt a slight thrill at being a part of this clandestine movement.

The drive from Khurashar took over two hours. And only for less than a quarter of that time were they on anything that even remotely resembled a road. The rest of the drive was over rocks, through sand, across meandering streams, and on ground so uneven that Harriet questioned how the jeep could possibly remain upright. Halfway through the drive she began thinking that the flight through the mountain pass hadn't been that bad after all.

The sun was low in the west when, seemingly in the midst of nowhere, the driver stopped the jeep and turned off the engine.

"Why are we stopping?"

"We are here."

Harriet looked around. "What do you mean we are here? I see nothing."

"It is good that you see nothing." Pulling a tarpaulin from under the backseat, the driver covered the jeep, blending the draped shape and gray-brown color into the rocky landscape. "Come."

After a walk of less than five minutes, they arrived at Kadar's headquarters. Harriet didn't see the cave openings until they were right in front of them, so well were they camouflaged.

"Is Adbul Kadan Kadar here?" Douglas asked. "Or will he be here?"

"The Imam is here."

Harriet took a deep breath. She was about to come face-to-face with Abdul Kadan Kadar, the man many thought was Satan personified. His most recent outrage, of course, was the attack on the football field in Tennessee, the bridges over the Mississipi River, and the DS Tower in Dallas. But over the past few years, Kadar's followers had also bombed an American Army barracks in Germany,

American embassies in Algeria and Pakistan, and a bus filled with American tourists in Egypt. Foiled plots to bomb the Lincoln and Holland Tunnels in New York, as well as the fifteen-thousand-member congregation of Prestonwood Baptist Church during a Sunday service in Dallas, were traced back directly to Abdul Kadan Kadar.

A small man, with a sand-colored pinched face, prominent nose, and gray beard, came to greet them. He was carrying an AK-47 rifle.

"Welcome to the headquarters of Islamic Jihad Muhahidin," he said. "I am Abdul Kadan Kadar. Come, we will eat. Then we will talk."

Twelve

Addison, Texas:

John and Don chose to eat at the Texas de Brazil restaurant, located on the corner of Addison and Beltline. It was a very good, if somewhat pricey, restaurant, and they chose it not only for the food, but also because of its proximity to the Addison Airport. Don had flown John and himself to Addison, which is a suburb of Dallas, where they were to meet Andy Garrison.

The deputy director of Homeland Security had flown to Addison in a chartered airplane, rather than a government plane, because he did not want to call attention to himself or to the meeting. John and Don met the Gulfstream IV, then took Andy a half mile down the street to the Texas de Brazil for lunch.

"First, let me thank you for the way you handled things at the DS Tower," Andy said.

"DS Tower?" John replied.

"I know you were the one called Satan," Andy said.

The conversation grew quiet as a waiter brought

around skewers of barbequed meat, including lamb, beef, pork, and chicken.

"You have your choice of meat, gentlemen," the waiter said.

"What is our limit?" Don asked.

"Oh, there is no limit, sir."

"Good. I'll take the lamb."

The waiter started to slide off a sizable portion of meat.

"No," Don said. "I mean I'll take the whole skewer."

"The whole skewer?" the waiter asked in surprise.

"Yes, and a couple of pieces of beef, a couple of pork, and a couple of chicken."

"Sir, that is a prodigious amount of meat."

"I can have more if I want it, right?"

The waiter shook his head in amazement, then began sliding the meat off until Don's plate was filled. It took a second plate for his garlic mashed potatoes, and still a third for his visit to the long, hundred-item salad bar.

"So, what's up?" John asked as they started their meal.

"We have a situation," Andy said.

"What kind of situation?"

"The kind of situation that I think only someone like your group can handle."

"We don't work for the government," John said.

"I know you don't. In fact, there are very few in the government who even know about you," Andy said. "But I know about you, and I know that you were the ones who took care of the situation in Dallas." Andy looked at Don. "And Don, the stock market could have taken a major hit as a result of the attacks, but somehow, it was stabilized. That has your fingerprints all over it."

"Damn, this lamb is good," Don said.

Andy sighed, and shook his head. "All right, all right, we won't discuss old news. But as I said, a situation is unfolding even as we speak. It's got to be taken care of, and taken care of quickly."

"This . . . situation . . . you are talking about. There's no government agency to handle it?" John asked.

Andy shook his head. "I'm afraid not. This is the kind of thing that only someone like you can handle."

"Someone like us?" John asked.

"Someone whose every move isn't subject to scrutiny."

"What are we talking about?"

Don opened his briefcase and took out a small video camera. He connected an earpiece to it, then handed the camera across the table to John. "There is a tape in the camera. Play it back, and watch the monitor."

John put the earpiece in his ear, then hit play and watched on the tiny, monitor screen.

The first person he saw was Douglas Sharbell.

"Why should I get eyestrain watching this guy?" John asked, looking up. "I won't even watch him on a big screen."

"Please, just watch," Andy said.

John turned his attention back to the tiny monitor. Sharbell was smiling into the camera.

"This is Douglas Sharbell. The United States

Government would pay twenty-five million dollars to anyone who can do what I am about to do. I am in a secret location"—he looked around—"so secret that I don't even know where it is. Even though I can't tell you where I am, I can tell you that this is the camp, the headquarters if you will, of Abdul Kadan Kadar. That's right, ladies and gentlemen, I am about to bring you an exclusive interview with the most sought-after man in the world, Abdul Kadan Kadar."

As Sharbell continued his setup, an arm came into the picture. The arm was behind Sharbell, and Sharbell, who was speaking into the camera, saw neither the arm, nor the curved knife that was in the hand.

Shockingly, the knife made a quick slashing motion across the front of Sharbell's neck, and blood began gushing forth like a fountain. The expression on Sharbell's face turned from one of arrogant achievement, to surprise, to horror, all in less than a second. Then, even as he fell, his eyes were rolling back into his head.

"Holy shit!" John said in surprise. He turned it off and looked up at Andy. "Is this for real?"

"It is very real," Andy said.

"How did you get this tape?"

"It was sent to us."

"To you? The Homeland Security Office?"

"No, it was mailed directly to POTUS. We got it after the White House staff, and ultimately the President of the United States himself, screened it."

"Sharbell always was a dumb son of a bitch," John said. "And I can't say that I'm shocked to see him get himself in a situation like this. But he was *our* dumb son of a bitch, and Abdul Kadan Kadar had no right to kill him."

"Turn it on again," Andy said. "There is more."

John punched the playback switch. This time he saw the face of Abdul Kadan Kadar.

"President Emerson. Let this serve as a warning to you. What you have just seen happen to America's most popular journalist will happen to any American who sets foot anywhere on our holy ground, and that means all Muslim countries. You will not be safe, even in those countries you consider your friends. We will kill all Americans, and if you send your soldiers after us, we will kill them too."

John shook his head. "This is just the usual rhetoric," he said.

"Wait," Andy replied. "There is more."

"And now," Kadar continued on tape, "we have a great prize. We have as our prisoner Senator Harriet Clayton."

The camera panned over to show Harriet Clayton, her eyes wide in panic, a knife held to her throat.

"I have two demands to make of you, Mr. Emerson. My first demand is that you immediately halt the bombing of our innocent women and children. Do you think your bombs hurt me? Do you think your bombs hurt the brave martyrs of the Islamic Jihad Muhahidin? They do not. They fall on defenseless villages. My second demand is that you return the money that was stolen from the account of the Islamic Jihad Muhahidin," Kadar said. "Return the money, all the money. When our account is credited with two billion dollars, the billion you stole, plus one billion dollars in interest, we will release Senator Clayton. If you do not do this, Senator Clayton will be killed, and her blood will be on your hands."

There was an inaudible comment, off camera, and Harriet shook her head, licked her lips, then looked into the camera.

"Mr. President," Harriet said. "I beg of you to do what Abdul Kadan Kadar asks. He is a reasonable man who is fighting for the freedom of his people. We have no right to be in this part of the world. We have no right to be bombing the innocent citizens of Sitarkistan. Our country is large, powerful, and arrogant. We are at fault here, we are the aggressors. We have defiled their holy places, we have diluted their religion with our capitalist and godless system. It is time we learned to live with our fellow-man, rather than attempt to make slaves of them."

John turned off the tape. "She is saying that now to save her life. But she has been spreading that same kind of liberal bullshit ever since she got into politics. She doesn't believe it now, she didn't believe it then. She is a whore, whether it be for votes or her life."

"Yes, that may well be," Andy agreed. "But as you said, she is *our* whore. And we can't just sit by and do nothing. We can't let her be killed."

"Are you telling me that the CIA can do nothing about this?"

"As an official government entity, there are limits to what they are allowed to do. The same thing applies to our military. Ironically, some of the most restrictive rules and regulations were championed by Senator Clayton herself."

"You folks do have yourselves in a bit of a bind, don't you?"

"Unfortunately, we do. That's why I've come to you."

"What, exactly, would you have us do?"

"Try and get Senator Clayton back, in one piece if possible."

"No interference?"

"I can promise you that there will be no interference," Andy said. "You understand, of course, that if anything goes wrong, POTUS will deny any knowledge of your existence. And since only a few of us do know about you, that denial will be convincing."

Even while eating, Don had been following the conversation, and now he stuck the earplug in his ear and played back what John had watched. John drummed his fingers on the table.

"Do you have any idea when the tape was made?"

"We believe the tape was made two days ago," Andy said. "Although Senator Clayton's trip was secret, and totally unauthorized, we now know that she left the country four days ago."

"For all we know, they could've killed her immediately after making this tape," John said.

"That is true."

"So no matter what we do, we may not be able to save her."

"That is also true."

John stroked his chin. "If we get involved in this thing, it won't be a half-assed operation. We will take care of that bastard Kadar once and for all. POTUS does understand that, doesn't he?"

"Understand it? He is counting on it," Andy said.

John nodded. "All right, let me get back to the others. This isn't a decision I'm going to make by myself." He chuckled sardonically. "Truth is, nearly everyone on the Code Name Team would probably just as soon see that woman stay over there. It's going to be hard to convince them to come to her rescue."

"I understand," Andy said.

John stood up. "We'll have the answer for you in six hours," he said.

"Your country thanks you, your President thanks you, and I thank you," Andy said.

"I hope you remember all this gratitude if I come to you for help."

Andy put up his right hand. "You have my word. Whatever you need, to the degree that it can be done, will be done."

When John and Don returned to the Code Name headquarters, Jennifer, Linda, and Wagner were watching TV in the living room. Eddie Clayton was on the screen, his expression one of concern. The words at the bottom of the screen read: *Edward Clayton, former Vice President of the United States.*

Clayton pointed to one of the gathered reporters. "Yes, you have a question?" he asked.

"Mr. Vice President, if you had won the election, is there anything you would have done differently that might have prevented this from happening?"

"Perhaps I would have been more receptive to the legitimate complaints of those people who feel that we, by our wealth and power, are a threat to their existence."

"What would you have done differently?"

Clayton paused for a moment, looking thoughtful, then, as though reluctant to speak, continued. "The President has made it clear that he will not negotiate with Abdul Kadan Kadar under any circumstances. I would have established a dialogue with him, to try and find a peaceful solution to the problems that divide us."

"But isn't establishing a dialogue exactly what Douglas Sharbell and your wife were trying to do?" another reporter asked. "And as you can see, it had disasterous consequences."

"Sharbell was a journalist, my wife is a Senator without the backing of the Administration," Eddie said. "My wife is a brave and dedicated woman who undertook this mission at great personal risk, in order to do what she could to defuse this smoldering situation. But without the backing of the current Administration, I'm afraid the mission never had a chance."

"Mr. Vice President, did you know your wife planned to meet with Kadar?"

Eddie shook his head. "No, I did not know. The mission was so sensitive that she had to keep it secret, even from me. Had I known about her mission, I would have attempted to talk her out of it, or barring that, attempted to secure support and backing from the Administration."

"Are you concerned for your wife's safety?"

"Yes, of course I am concerned. I think that, at

the very minimum, we should have an immediate halt to all bombing operations."

"Do you think we should pay the two billion dollars Kadar is asking for?"

"Well, that's not for me to say," Eddie replied. "Two billion dollars is an awful lot of money and the President probably could not, personally, authorize such a payment. It would take an emergency session of Congress to do that, and I don't see it happening."

John picked up the remote and clicked the picture off.

"Hey, what'd you do that for?" Jennifer asked.

"We need to talk."

"About what?"

"About that," John said, pointing to the screen. "About Senator Clayton."

"So, that's why you went to meet Andy Garrison," Linda said. "I wondered what that mysterious trip was all about."

"We've been asked to rescue her," John said.

"Rescue her? Ha! If I had my way, Kadar would make her one of the wives in his harem," Linda said.

"Yeah, she would like that, wouldn't she?" Jennifer asked. "Being with all those women?" Jennifer rubbed her eyebrow with her little finger, and the others laughed.

"What did you say to Mr. Garrison?" Wagner asked.

"I told him I would get back to him. I'm not going to make a commitment without everyone's backing."

"I say let her stew in her own juices," Linda said. "Nobody asked her to go over there."

"You don't really mean that," Jennifer said.

Linda sighed, and shook her head. "No, not really," she admitted.

"The question is not *will* we do it, but *can* we do it?" John said. "Finding her isn't going to be easy, and once we do find her, rescuing her is going to be even harder."

"Do you think you can do it?" Wagner asked.

"I don't know," John said. "It would be a challenge."

"I'm willing to accept the challenge," Don said.

Jennifer smiled. "I've never known any of us to walk away from a challenge," she said.

"I'll say this," Wagner put in. "If you can pull this off, we're going to pile up more favors in high places than we'll ever be able to call in."

"Yes, well, before we jump in, we should consider the fact that we would be working for the government," Linda said. "I left the LAPD because of all the restrictions and PC bullshit they were putting on us. The federal government is worse, as I'm sure all of you know."

John and Don had worked with the CIA, while Jennifer was a former FBI agent.

"Andy Garrison promised us hands off," John said.

"Do you really trust the government?" Linda asked.

"No," John answered. "But I've known Andy Garrison for a long time, and I do trust him."

"Well, if you trust Garrison, I trust you. If you say go, I'm ready," Linda said.

"I am too," Jennifer added.

"Now that that is decided, when do we eat?" Don asked.

The others laughed.

Washington, D.C., the Oval Office:

"Mr. President, when you get a moment, I'd like a word with you," Andy said.

"Of course, of course," the President replied. "Come on in, Andy. You know the former Vice President."

Andy had not noticed Eddie Clayton sitting in the President's office until now, and he nodded at him. "Mr. Vice President," he said.

"What is it, Andy?" asked the President.

"I'll, uh, come back later," Andy said, looking pointedly at Eddie Clayton.

"Oh, I see. Well, there is no need for you to come back later. I'm sure Eddie would excuse us for a moment."

"Mr. President, is this about my wife?" Eddie asked.

"I'm not at liberty to say."

"Oh, for Chrissake, Bill," Eddie exploded. "You of all people should know what I'm going through right now. Your own wife was in a similar situation not too long ago."

"Yes, she was." The President did not say, though he could have, that his wife was an accidental victim, whereas Harriet Clayton had put herself in jeopardy.

"If you are talking contingency plans that concern her, I would like to listen in."

"I'll keep you informed," the President said, but he stared pointedly, meaning that he still wanted the former Vice President to leave.

Finally getting the hint, Eddie cleared his throat, then nodded. "Yes, please do. I would appreciate that, Mr. President," he said.

"Stop by any time, Eddie. I always enjoy our visits. You know, the Indians used to measure their wealth not only by their allies, but by their adversaries. I believe I was enriched by your opposition in the campaign."

"Yes, as do I. Good day, Mr. President."

"Good day."

Andy stood quietly until the former Vice President was gone.

"Have a seat," President Emerson offered.

"Thanks."

Andy sat on the end of the gold couch; the President sat in a gold chair. The floor was covered with a dark blue carpet, representing the seal of the President.

Outside the door, unheard by either of them, a Secret Service agent spoke into his radio.

"The former Vice President has departed. Andrew Garrison is now with POTUS."

"What have you got, Andy?" the President asked.

"I've made contact with the Code Name Team. They will do it."

"Good," President Emerson said. He sighed. "Now the question is, *can* they do it?"

"I won't guarantee that they can," Andy said. "But I will tell you this. If it is humanly possible for this to be done, these people will pull it off."

"You have that much confidence in them?"

"Yes, sir, I do."

The President shook his head. "I don't understand why we can't have people like that working for us."

"Oh, we do have good people working for the government, Mr. President. Some just as good as these people are. It isn't the quality of our personnel that is the problem, it is the insanity of our policies. Everything anyone does is subject to scrutiny and control by the GAO, Justice Department, and Congressional oversight committees."

"I see what you mean."

"I gave them our absolute guarantee that there would be no interference from us, no restrictions."

"All right."

Andy cleared his throat. "I also promised to support them with anything they asked for."

"How are we going to do that?" the President asked. "If they are 'off the books,' so to speak, if we start getting all these requests, how will we explain them?"

"I know how we can do it, if you are willing to take a personal risk."

"How is that?"

"You authorize everything I ask for through Homeland Security. As slow as everything moves, it will be several months before anyone figures out what is going on, and by that time we will have either succeeded or failed. If we have succeeded, your stock will be so high that nobody can touch you. If we fail, the only plea you can make when they start coming after you is you had to do something."

"That would be a pretty weak response."

"Yes, Mr. President. It would be."

"We'll just have to not fail."

"Yes, sir, that's the way I look at it as well."

President Emerson stroked his chin for a moment as he considered what Andy just told him.

"You want to know what really upsets me, Andy? The fact that the people who are going to come after me hardest will be the people in Clayton's own party. And Edward J. Clayton himself will undoubtedly lead the charge."

"Yes, sir, he will, and will probably garner enough sympathy votes over the loss of his dear wife that he'll be a shoo-in for the nomination, and a strong opponent at the next election."

"Yes, I know," the President said. He chuckled. "I just wish the payoff was greater, like the rescue of some movie star or sports hero."

"I agree, sir."

"All right, Andy, let's go for broke," the President said. "Anything you need, you call me. I will tell Dorothy to put you through, no matter what, even if I am on another line."

"Yes, sir," Andy said. "Thank you, sir."

"And let's just pray to God that this works."

Andy laughed. "Perhaps we should also pray that God doesn't have the same negative feelings about Harriet Clayton that we have."

The President laughed as well. "Andy, you are incorrigible," he said.

Thirteen

*At sea, aboard the Liberian-flagged
ship* George V. Gaffey:

Built in 1975, the *Gaffey* was a bulk cargo carrier
that displaced 37,000 tons. It was 344 feet long,
sixty-four feet at the beam, and drew twenty-five
feet. Its six-thousand-horsepower steam-turbine engines could push it through the water at fifteen
knots, though for the last two days it had been pro-
ceeding at less than six knots. Indeed, if anyone
flying over that part of the ocean at this particular
moment would happen to look down, they would
see a red and white ship moving so slowly that it appeared to be a painted vessel upon a painted sea.

Holds one through three were filled with used
farm machinery, which according to the bill of lad-
ing was bound for Israel. Holds four and five were
sealed off from all but a few of the onboard personnel, and rumors ran rife throughout the ship as to
what those holds might contain. There were some
who insisted that they were carrying the remains of
the space craft that the U.S. Air Force had been stor-
ing in Area 51 since 1947. According to this theory
they would rendezvous with the flying saucer

"mother ship" somewhere in the middle of the Pacific Ocean. This was why their route had taken them considerably south of the normal trade routes. Also contributing to this hypothesis were the half-dozen large satellite dishes that sprouted from the afterdeck of the ship. These, the true believers insisted, were to allow contact with the aliens.

In addition to the satellite dishes, there was a veritable forest of antennae. Like holds four and five, the afterdeck was off-limits to all but a few of the technicians. The technicians, in their white jumpsuits, puttered around with wrenches, meters, and lubricants, tending to the satellite dishes and spiked antennae as if they were gardeners nursing their plants.

Two Filipino seamen, wearing only shorts and sandals, stood at the rail on the starboard deck amidships, smoking cigarettes while enjoying the relatively cool night air. Just below them, the bilge pipe began spewing water, giving an impression that the *Gaffey* was some great living beast, shamelessly relieving itself.

"Hector, do you ever wonder what is down there?" Ruben Cruz asked.

"Down where?"

"You know down where. In four and five. The place they call 'The Shack.'"

"I think it is nothing," Hector replied.

"Nothing? The way they watch over that place? And with all the antennae this ship has? I have never seen a ship with so many antennae."

Hector laughed. "Do you believe, as some of the others, that we are carrying a space ship?"

"I don't know what I believe," Ruben said. "Maybe this is true, I don't know."

"Only the foolish would believe such a thing. I think it is filled with special computers or something that they must be very careful with."

"No. It is more than that," Ruben insisted. "They have men with guns guarding the doors. If you try to go in, they will send you away. If you don't go away, I think they would shoot you."

"Why would you want to go in?"

"I am curious. Aren't you?"

Hector shook his head, then flipped his cigarette over the rail. The glowing orange ember made an arc down and back as it fell through the darkness toward the black sea. "I am paid not to be curious," he said. "This ship is paying at one and a half times scale."

"Yes, I am curious about that as well."

As the two seamen were discussing the makeup of the ship, John Barrone, Mike Rojas, Chris Farmer, Jennifer Barnes, and Linda Marsh were in the wardroom drinking coffee. Behind them, a bridge game was in progress, involving two of the ship's officers and two of the technicians who worked in The Shack. The technicians worked for Don Yee and were part of what the rest of the ship referred to as the "Nerd Herd."

John had augmented his team for the operation they were now referring to as "Quickstrike" by the addition of Mike and Chris.

A powerfully built, rather swarthy man, Mike

Rojas weighed approximately 180 pounds, and was forty years old. Formerly with the Internal Security Division of IRS, Mike often quipped that "nobody has ever liked me anyway, so the IRS was the place for me to be." Mike was of Mexican descent, and liked to point out that one of his ancestors died inside the Alamo, one of the few Texas-born defenders to do so.

The other addition to the operation team was Chris Farmer. Chris wasn't much of a talker, but he didn't have to be. A U.S. Army-trained sniper, Chris let his rifle talk for him. His rifle did talk for him during the Gulf War when he had seventeen confirmed kills, not one from closer than one thousand yards.

After he left the Army, Chris entered the Secret Service. He was ideal for the job, not only because of his ability with weapons, but because he was a big man, six feet, four inches tall, weighing in at 220 pounds.

One afternoon while he was on duty, Vice President Eddie Clayton asked Chris to stand guard outside his door and not let anyone in while he was "in conference." The Vice President was in conference with a young female intern. The next afternoon, the Vice President asked Chris to walk down the hall and tell that same intern that "the coast is clear."

Declaring that he had signed on to be a Secret Service agent and not a pimp, Chris submitted his resignation within the hour.

Don Yee was still part of the Quickstrike operation, but he would not be going into the field with John, Mike, Chris, Jennifer, and Linda. Instead, he buried himself in The Shack, where he had banks of computer terminals, video screens, radar units, radio transceivers, and other pieces of electronic equipment. From there, he could monitor military and commercial air and sea traffic anywhere in the world.

"Is Don not going to come up for air?" Jennifer asked.

"You know Don," John replied. "Give him a bank of computers . . ."

"And plenty of food," Mike put in. The others laughed.

"And he could stay down there for a month."

"Double," one of the cardplayers said from the bridge game that was going on behind them.

"Five no-trump, Wilson?" one of the other bridge-playing technicians said to his playing partner. "You can't be satisfied with book, you have to go to five?"

"You know me, Tony. I boldly go," Wilson replied as he pushed his horn-rimmed glasses back up his nose.

As Tony began laying out the cards for dummy, one of the ship's officers, who was playing with the two computer geeks, chuckled. "Oh, what a shame, Wilson," he said. "Tony has only two face cards, and you stand doubled."

"You could've been a little more help," Wilson complained. "I've no way to get to the table."

"You're the one who boldly goes," Tony replied. "If you want to slay windmills, who am I to stop you?" Getting up from the table, Tony poured himself a cup of coffee, then looked over at the Code Name Team.

"Where did you people come up with Don Yee?" Tony asked. "He is a genius with computers. Give him a powerful enough mainframe, and I do believe he could take over the world."

"Don't you fellas in the, uh . . ." Jennifer paused, but Tony finished for her.

"You can say it . . . Nerd Herd. It's a sobriquet we wear proudly."

Jennifer. "Yes, the Nerd Herd. Don't you fellas in the Nerd Herd give Don any ideas about taking over the world. He might just try it."

"Is it true that the radar on this ship can track any aircraft anywhere in the world?" Mike asked.

Tony shook his head. "No, the radar on this ship doesn't track it," he answered, "but by downloading from the appropriate satellite, we are able to read radar from any linked unit. You want to know what aircraft is on final approach at DFW, how many aircraft are crossing the Atlantic, or who's flying over Iraq? Even though we are sitting in the middle of the Pacific Ocean, all we have to do is call it up, and we can tell you."

"Well, answer this. How did the crew get the idea we are carrying a crashed space ship?" Chris asked.

Tony laughed. "That was Don's idea. He figured they were going to speculate about something, so he decided to give them something interesting to speculate about."

"The crew is in good company," one of the ship's officers added. "Neither of us knows what this voyage is all about." He had indicated the other ship's officer, who was his bridge partner. "The only members of the crew who do know are the captain and the first officer. All I can tell you with absolute certainty is that we damned sure aren't carrying farm equipment to Israel. By the way, Tony, you fellas are down three, doubled. I just wish the bold one here had redoubled."

Haifa, Israel:

John stood on deck, looking over the railing at the sparkling blue water of the harbor. An Israeli gunboat had intercepted the ship as it approached Haifa, ordering it to stand to until boarded for inspection.

"I wonder how long this is going to take," Mike said, coming up to stand alongside John.

"Shouldn't be too long now," John said. He pointed toward a boat approaching them. "And you can't really blame them. They've lived under the threat of attacks and suicide bombings ever since this country began."

"Yeah, I don't hold it against them," Mike said. "But I would like to get off the ship and get this thing going."

The approaching harbor boat pulled up alongside the ship; then three men came aboard, one officer and two armed seamen. They were greeted by the captain of the *Gaffey.*

"Good afternoon, Captain. I am Commander Zev Bin-Yashai. Do you have your papers?"

"We do," Captain Philbin said, showing the Israeli a packet of papers.

"What is your cargo?" Bin-Yashai asked as he began looking through the papers.

"Farm machinery," Captain Philbin answered.

"Are there any weapons on board?"

"Hello, Zev," John said, walking over to join the two men. "You've changed quite a bit since the last time I saw you."

"I beg your pardon?" Zev said, looking at John in confusion. Then, way back in the recesses of his mind, there was a glimmer of recognition. "Barrone?" Zev asked. "Are you John Barrone?"

"I am," John said, extending his hand. The two men shook hands, then embraced. "How is your mother?" he asked.

"She's fine, she's doing well, thank you," Zev said.

"Please tell her I asked about her. No, on second thought, don't tell her. I'm sure she blames me for leading your father astray."

Zev shook his head. "No, my father managed to do that on his own, thank you. If he hadn't teamed up with you, he would've found some other outlet for his thirst for adventure . . . among other things."

"Captain Philbin, if you would, show these two men the farm equipment," John said. "Commander Bin-Yishai and I have some catching up to do."

"Uh, Mr. Barrone, I really should see for myself," Zev said.

"And you shall, you shall," John said. "But first, I would like a few minutes of your time. It's very important."

Zev thought about the proposition for a moment, then nodded. "All right," he said. "I'll give you a few minutes."

John walked toward the bow, opening up some space between him and the others, and by that action, inviting Zev to join him.

"What's this about, Mr. Barrone?" Zev asked. "I'm sure you aren't bringing me up here to talk about old times. If you recall, the old times aren't that pleasant for me. My dad left my mother, she divorced him, and he wound up getting killed in Monaco. They said it was robbery and murder, but I never bought that. I'm sure it had something to do with the kind of work he was doing for you."

John sighed. "It wasn't robbery and murder. It was a revenge killing. He was killed by Mehdi Al Ahmed."

Zev nodded. "I thought it was something like that."

"If there is any consolation to the fact, Al Ahmed is dead."

"Why do I think you killed him?"

"Maybe you're just perceptive that way."

"You did kill him, didn't you?"

"Yes."

"What's going on, John?" Zev asked. He nodded toward the ship. "I can't really see someone like you being involved with a shipment of farm machinery."

John was glad Zev called him John, rather than Mr. Barrone. That meant he had made some progress with the young man.

"You are aware that Abdul Kadan Kadar has captured Senator Harriet Clayton?" John asked.

"Are you kidding? The Arabs are dancing in the streets in celebration."

John chuckled. "So are the political conservatives in my country."

Zev laughed with him. "What does that have to do with this ship?"

"Everything," John replied. He pointed toward the antennae at the ship's stern. "We are loaded down with surveillance and monitoring equipment," he said.

"Well, why didn't you just come right out and say so?" Zev asked. "If your government has clearance from my government for all of this . . ."

John held up his hand to stop him. He shook his head. "This isn't a government operation."

"What? You've got all this equipment and it isn't a government operation?"

"No," John said.

"Does your government know you are here?"

"No," John replied. He knew that Andy Garrison, and by extension the President, knew that he was here. But he knew also that they would need to be able to hang onto the concept of credible deniability. Therefore, he couldn't say that this operation was sanctioned, or even known.

"I don't understand. If your government doesn't know you are here, why are you here?"

"I'm here because I have to be here. And I need your help."

Zev shook his head. "I don't know what you want me to do, but I will not violate my oath."

"I neither expect nor want you to do that," John said. "All I want you to do is put the ship on a twenty-four-hour hold, then deny us docking privileges. Send us back to sea."

"Now I know there is more to it than that," Zev said. "That makes absolutely no sense whatever."

"That's all I'm asking," John said. "A twenty-four-hour hold in place, then deny us the right to dock."

"And this will help you?"

"Yes. It will help more than you can know, or need to know."

Zev took the small radio from his belt. "Moshe, Aryeh, come back to the deck."

Zev walked back to Captain Philbin, arriving at about the same time the two Israeli inspectors returned to the deck. "Captain Philbin, I am ordering you to remain right here, without moving, for twenty-four hours," Zev said.

"And then?" Captain Philbin asked.

Zev looked over at John. "At the end of the twenty-four-hour period, you will get further instructions."

"What am I to do with the farm equipment?"

"As far as I'm concerned, you can dump it into the sea," Zev said. "Which is what I expect you intended to do all along."

"Very good, sir," Captain Philbin said, without commenting on Zev's rather caustic observation.

That night, Haifa Harbor:

Dressed in black wetsuits, John, Mike, Chris, Jennifer, and Linda went into the water at 1:05 A.M. All five were equipped with submersible propulsion devices, and by hanging onto the little underwater scooters, they moved quickly away from the *Gaffey*, steering a course of two-nine-five for one half hour. When they surfaced, they saw an Israeli fishing boat. John flashed a light toward the boat, and the boat flashed back. Fifteen minutes later the submersibles were at the bottom of the sea, and John and his team were on board the boat. They checked the gear equipment in their waterproof bags and found that it was none the worse for wear.

Fourteen

New York, Eddie Clayton's apartment:

Eddie Clayton stood at the window of his apartment looking out over the huge black slabs and sparkling lights of Manhattan. Behind him, mixing drinks at the bar, was Henry Norton.

"I can't believe you let her go over there," Eddie said.

"You can't believe *I* let her go? I'm just her AA. You are her husband. Why did *you* let her go?"

Eddie turned away from the window. "Because I didn't know anything about it, that's why."

"Yes, well, I knew she was going, but I couldn't talk her out of it. And if you are truthful with yourself, you will admit that, even if you had known, you couldn't have prevented it. She was dead set to go and there was nothing short of arresting her that would have stopped her."

Eddie sighed. "Yeah," he said. "I guess you're right. The bitch has sure grandstanded me this time, hasn't she?"

Henry chuckled as he brought two drinks away from the bar and handed one of them to the former Vice President.

"Your concern for her safety touches me."

"Knock it off, Henry. You know how it is between us," Eddie growled.

"I do," he said. "You say she grandstanded you, but on the other hand, she may be hoist by her own petard."

"How so?" Eddie asked.

"First, let me ask you something. How would you react if the worst happened?"

"The worst?"

"If she didn't come back."

"The truth?" Eddie replied. He took a swallow of his drink before he continued. "As far as I'm concerned, the dumb bitch got herself into this mess. I'd probably go somewhere and celebrate."

Henry chuckled, then shook his head. "No," he said. "That's not how you feel at all. You admire her for having the courage to attempt to open a dialogue with Kadar, and you are deeply concerned over her safety. You don't want to say or do anything that would interfere with whatever program or operation the President may have in mind. But you do intend to monitor the situation closely. After all, it is your wife there now. This has gotten personal."

"You're full of shit, Henry. You know I don't feel that way at all."

"Oh, but you do," Henry said. He held up a finger to keep Eddie from responding as he walked over to the coffee table to open his briefcase. He took out a packet of papers and showed them to Eddie. "Do you know what these are?"

Eddie shook his head. "I haven't the foggiest notion."

"These are your poll numbers as of last night. For the first time since the election, your numbers are competitive with POTUS."

"What?" Eddie asked, reaching for the papers. "But why? How? I don't understand."

"It's simple. You're pulling in the sympathy vote. The public sees you as the loving husband of a brave woman who is now in danger because of Emerson's failed foreign policies."

"I'll be damned."

"Tomorrow, you are having a prayer meeting with the Reverend Jeremy Johnson."

"What the hell do I want with that self-serving blowhard?"

"That self-serving blowhard is good for about ten million black votes," Henry said.

Eddie put the papers back down and looked at Henry. "I don't understand you," he said. "Three days ago you had all but written off my candidacy. You were pimping for Harriet."

"Three days ago Harriet Clayton was a viable candidate," Henry said. "But she's taken herself out of the picture. And in so doing, she's brought you back."

"What if she comes back in one piece?"

"If she does, her stock will be higher than either yours or the President's."

"I see."

Henry held up his finger. "Ah, but if she doesn't come back, if she is, God forbid, killed by Kadar, your numbers will go through the roof. You will win the Presidency in a walk."

"Why are you helping me?"

"Because I am a pragmatist," Henry said.

"Uh-huh. And the next question is, why would I want you to help me?"

"Because I'm good and you know it. I can help you win. Think of the combination, the late Senator Clayton's bereaved husband and her loyal AA, teaming up to right the terrible wrong that took her life."

"What if she doesn't die? What if she comes back?"

"Then all bets are off, and I go back to working for her."

Eddie took another drink, studying Henry over the rim on his glass. "You can see, can't you, how that might make it difficult for me to trust you?"

"Frankly, no, I can't see. Eddie, I am being very candid with you. There are no surprises with me. I should think that would be worth something."

"It is."

"Then I'm working for you?"

"You are," Eddie said with a nod.

"And you will listen to what I say, do what I tell you to do?"

"Yes."

"Good." Henry walked over to the bedroom door.

"Wait, where are you going?" Eddie asked.

Henry looked back at Eddie, and again held up his finger as if saying, "Wait, and you will see." He jerked the door open.

"Ahhh!" Ginger screamed.

"Put your clothes on, honey," Henry said. "The Vice President won't be needing your services for a while."

Ginger, who was standing totally naked alongside the bed, looked through the door toward Eddie.

"Do as he says," Eddie said.

Henry turned back to Eddie. "Don't get caught with any fluff. I mean it. It is more important now than it has ever been, do you understand? From now until the election, you have to be the loving husband, either worried about the fate of your wife, or grieving over the fact that she is dead."

"All right," Eddie said.

"I mean it, Eddie," Henry reiterated. "One indiscretion, just one, will blow everything. If you have to, tie a knot in your pecker. I don't want it to come out of your pants for anything but a piss."

"I'll watch myself," Eddie said.

Henry shook his head. "No, that's not good enough. I don't want you to watch yourself. That implies that you will be careful. Well, you can't 'be careful,' do you understand? If you do anything, you will be caught, and that will be the end of it. I want you to swear to me now that you will have nothing to do with any woman until after all this is over."

Eddie nodded. "All right," he said. "I swear."

Ginger came out of the bedroom then, fully dressed.

"Where are you going, honey? I'll drop you off," Henry promised.

"I have an apartment on sixty-sixth," she said.

Taking Ginger by the arm, Henry led her to the door. Just before he left, he turned back to Eddie.

"I've made arrangements for your prayer meeting with the Reverend Johnson to be televised," Henry said. "I'll pick you up tomorrow."

Camp of Abdul Kadan Kadar:

"Would you like some tea, Mrs. Clayton?"

Harriet had heard the one making an offer of tea addressed as Farid. Whether that was a first or last name, she didn't know. He did seem to exercise some degree of authority, though, because others acquiesced to his orders.

"It's *Senator* Clayton, you asshole," Harriet said. "And no, I don't want any of your goddamned tea. Don't you have anything real to drink around here? Whiskey? Beer?"

"Our religion does not allow us to imbibe spirits," Farid replied.

"Not even wine?"

"When we get to heaven, we will be rewarded with fine wine, and with seventy-two virgins."

Harriet looked at him with an expression of confusion, then laughed out loud. "Wait a minute, no wine on earth, but you can have it when you get to heaven?"

"That is our teaching."

"And seventy-two virgins? Where the hell do they come from?"

"Allah will provide them."

"And what do the women get when they go to heaven?"

"They will have the privilege of serving their men," Farid said.

Harriet shook her head. "You know what I think? I think you are as full of shit as a Christmas turkey."

"Are all American women as foul-mouthed as you are?" Farid asked.

"The ones who have balls are."

"Balls?" Farid asked, clearly confused.

"Gonads. Testicles," Harriet said.

"Testicles? American women have testicles?"

"Jesus, don't you have any concept of metaphor?" Harriet asked. She stood up. "I have to pee."

Farid said something in a language Harriet couldn't understand. One of the guards left the cave, then returned a moment later with two women. Only the eyes of the women could be seen, but both were carrying guns.

"They will go with you," Farid said.

"Let's go, ladies," Harriet said. "The good American Senator has to take a piss, and if you're nice to me, I'll let you watch."

Washington, D.C.:

"Could you give me a white balance?" a cameraman asked, and a technician held a white square in front of the camera while the camera was adjusted. Another moved to the podium and did a sound check.

"Can you hear me, George?"

The sound engineer put his finger to the speaker in his ear.

"Yes, I can hear you."

"I need to take a pee."

George laughed. "You know what your mother always used to tell you. You should've thought of that before we started. Now you'll just have to wait."

"Yeah, but for how long? You've done shoots with Jeremy Johnson before. He is one long-winded son of a bitch."

The sound and the three cameras were part of the pool, feeding audio and video to nearly a dozen network and cable news services. As a result, there were twenty or more reporters from both electronic and print media gathered at the gate in front of the White House.

Henry Norton had given a great deal of consideration as to where to hold the press conference, finally deciding on the gate in front of the White House as the most dramatic staging. In so doing he sought to emphasize the point that the current mess was being presided over by President Bill Emerson, the suggestion being that if Eddie Clayton were on the other side of the White House gates, the country would not be in such a mess. It would also remind everyone that Eddie Clayton was still a viable candidate for President.

Henry left nothing to chance. He rounded up several activists and had them standing by to greet Eddie when he arrived. They were carrying signs, all of which had been carefully screened and approved.

MR. PRESIDENT, STOP THE BOMBING NOW!

*HOW MANY MORE INNOCENT PEOPLE
MUST DIE?*

CITIZENS FOR A PEACEFUL SOLUTION!

I VOTED FOR EDDIE CLAYTON!

A car arrived in front of the White House, and though it was escorted by the police, it wasn't a limousine. It was a Ford Crown Victoria, a nice automobile, but not overstated. This too was part of Henry Norton's carefully prepared presentation, to show that Eddie Clayton was a man of the people, rather than a part of the government-caused problem.

Eddie got out of the car first, followed by Jeremy Johnson. The spectators began applauding as Eddie and the Reverend Johnson walked toward the cameras.

Graciously, Eddie held his hand toward the podium and the bank of microphones, inviting Johnson to speak.

Johnson adjusted the microphone, then leaned into it and began to speak in the sonorous, almost melodic tone that had become his trademark.

"It is time for the great nation of America to put an end to the spiraling violence that is going on between the world's three great religions. Mr. President, stop the bombing now."

"Stop the bombing!" the crowd replied.

"Stop the bombing!"

"Stop the bombing!"

Jeremy Johnson smiled and nodded his head while they chanted, then held up his hands and the crowd grew quiet.

"Senator Harriet Clayton went to the Middle East

to speak with Imam Abdul Kadan Kadar. I wish I could tell you that she took with her a message of peace, a message of hope, but I cannot tell you that. The only thing Harriet Clayton took with her was her own courage and goodness of heart, because there was no message of peace from President Emerson. And now, any hope that Harriet might have engendered with her brave mission has been all but extinguished by President Emerson's military response to every provocation.

"I urge the President to now give weight to the ill-fated mission of the brave Madame Senator from New Jersey, to respond to terror, not by causing the innocent to suffer beneath the rubble caused by American bombs, but by extending the olive branch of peace, and stop the bombing."

"Stop the bombing!"

"Stop the bombing!"

"Stop the bombing!"

Again, Jeremy let the crowd continue to chant for several seconds before calling for quiet.

"The Emerson Administration has not spoken with one voice on the issues at hand," Johnson said, resuming his speech. "This lack of clarity creates confusion," he said. "And that confusion has resulted in the deaths of so many innocent people, at the football stadium in Tennessee, on the bridges that cross the Mississippi River, and under the pile of rubble in the Muslim towns and cities that have felt the weight of our bombs. These, my friends, are the wages of an impotent foreign policy. Now I'll be glad to take any questions."

As the reporters began shouting questions to the

charismatic black leader, Eddie leaned toward Henry and shielded his words with his hand.

"What the hell is that grandstanding son of bitch doing taking questions?" Eddie asked. "Doesn't he understand this is *my* press conference?"

"Don't worry about it," Henry said. "It will all work out."

"I hope so. I'd hate to think I teamed up with that arrogant bastard for nothing."

"Reverend Johnson, did you counsel with the Vice President about his wife?"

"I did," Johnson replied.

"What did you tell him?"

"I told him to put his faith in God. Then we prayed together. Then I told him to keep hope alive."

"Have you heard from Abdul Kadan Kadar?" one of the other reporters asked.

"Me? No, I'm not a government official."

"But you have had some success in brokering the release of American hostages before. Would you talk with him if he made the overture?"

"Yes, of course I would." As if just getting the idea, Johnson stared into the camera. "Imam Abdul Kadan Kadar, I have a feeling you will see this news conference. If you do, I beg of you now, in the name of the one God both our great religions worship, let this good woman go. If you must hold a hostage, then I ask that you take me."

"Oh, for crying out loud," Eddie groaned quietly. "Now he has offered to exchange himself for Harriet."

"Reverend Johnson, are you saying you would

volunteer to become a hostage?" one of the reporters shouted.

"Yes, if it meant the release of my sister in Christ, Senator Harriet Clayton."

Some of the other reporters began shouting questions then, but Johnson held up his hands to stop them.

"Please," he said, "I've hogged the microphone enough. The man who needs our support now is the former Vice President. Mr. Eddie Clayton."

Johnson stepped away and, making a sweeping gesture with his arm, turned the podium over to Eddie.

Eddie walked toward the podium, forcing a smile.

"I thank the Reverend Johnson for his kind words, his counseling, and his prayers," Eddie said. "And I ask for the prayers of all Americans, not only for the safety of my dear wife, but for those innocent men, women, and children whose only crime is to live in a place where American bombs are falling."

Oval Office:

President Emerson was drinking a cup of coffee as he watched Eddie Clayton's news conference. He chuckled.

"Old Eddie looks about as comfortable with Jeremy Johnson as I would," Emerson said.

"Yes, I'll just bet he wished he hadn't opened that box," Andy replied. "On the other hand, their call for an immediate halt of the bombing is playing right into our hands."

"How is that?" the President asked.

"I've been in touch with the Code Name Team. They are going tonight, but they have asked for a temporary halt in the bombing, an envelope that will allow them to get in and out."

"I don't know," Emerson said, stroking his chin. "I hate easing up on those bastards, even for a moment."

"Look at it this way, Mr. President. You aren't easing up on them, you are just using a different weapon. I was concerned that they might be suspicious of a temporary bombing halt. But now, we can do it and it will look as if we are taking Eddie Clayton's suggestion."

"Sort of a peace initiative?" Emerson asked.

"Yes, sir. A twenty-four-hour cessation in the bombing. That will give our team plenty of time to get in and out, and the peace initiative ploy will be a credible reason."

"All right, do it," Emerson said.

Henry Norton insisted that Vice President Eddie Clayton move to his Washington house, at least for the duration of the crisis concerning his wife.

"Let's face it," Henry said. "As far as national politics is concerned, this is the center of the known universe. And your coming here will show everyone how concerned you are about the fate of the Senator."

"The Senator," Eddie replied with a snort. "I got

her that seat. If she hadn't married me, she would still be chasing ambulances somewhere."

"That may be so," Henry agreed. "But however she got there, she is there. And you are going to speak with every reporter we can find, from a ten-watt radio station in rural New Mexico to *Meet the Press.* Your job is to keep yourself in the public eye."

It required little more than a suitcase for Eddie to move back to the Washington, so he complied with Henry's recommendation, taking up residence in Harriet's house. It accomplished just what Henry said it would, in that Eddie became a frequent guest on television and radio shows, as well as the subject of numerous articles. In the meantime, his poll numbers continued to climb.

Eddie had just finished another interview, and one of the sound technicians was removing his lavalier microphone, when Jim Neighbors, the show's host, leaned over to talk to him.

"It was a good interview," he said.

"Thanks."

"I would love to have asked you about the rescue operation, but of course couldn't, for fear of jeopardizing its success. Off camera, though, I am interested in your take on it."

Eddie knew nothing of any rescue operation, but he was also politically savvy enough not to let on that he was in the dark.

"Well, obviously, I hope it is successful," he said.

"What do you think about the fact that it is a renegade group?" Neighbors asked.

"I'd hardly call them renegades," Eddie said. He had no idea what Neighbors was talking about.

"What would you call them? They aren't associated with any government agency. The way I hear it, our government has hired a team of mercenaries to do the job."

"Where are you getting all this information?"

Neighbors held out his hand. "I know, I know, it's top-secret stuff. But I am a reporter, you know, and a damn good one if I say so myself. I do have my sources."

"Yes, well, I hope you are careful with these sources," Eddie said. "I wouldn't want to think that the operation failed because someone compromised it."

Neighbors laid his finger across his lips. "Don't worry about me," he said. "My lips are sealed. The only reason I mentioned it to you is because you already knew about it."

"I don't know anything about it, I swear I don't," Henry Norton replied when Eddie asked him about the rescue operation.

"I wonder what he meant by the fact that this was a mercenary operation."

Henry shook his head. "I don't know the answer to that one either."

"Well, maybe it's time you found out about it."

Henry lit a cigarette, took a puff, then exhaled, studying Eddie across the cloud of smoke through narrowed eyes before he answered.

"Find out about it? Or stop it?" he asked.

"You can stop it?" Eddie replied quickly, then checked himself. "I mean, what do you mean, stop it?"

Henry chuckled. "I know what you mean," he said. "The question is, do you want the rescue effort stopped?"

"No, of course not. Not if it has any chance of success," Eddie said.

"I know what you mean," Henry said. "Although, if she suddenly showed up, it would throw a monkey wrench into everything I've done for you."

"That wouldn't be a problem for you, would it? You said that if she came back home, her poll numbers would be higher than mine."

"Yeah, I said that. And I believed it when I said it. But it's a funny thing. Your numbers just keep going higher, while hers have dipped. Seems a lot of people think she has put the U.S. in this crisis by her own irrational behavior. And, of course, there has always been that negative thing about her. Even when her positive numbers were high, her negative numbers were almost as high. Now, with her negative numbers up and her positive numbers down, she has become a political liability."

"So what you are saying is, you are committing to me?"

Henry nodded. "Yeah," he said. "I'm committing to you. So the question remains, what do you want me to do?"

"What do I want you to do about what?"

"About the rescue attempt?"

"Here is the thing about me, Henry," Eddie said. "Once I turn a campaign over to my manager, I keep hands off." He held up both hands to illustrate his point. "Do you understand what I mean? It's your ballgame, to play any way you want."

"I understand," Henry said with a small smile.

Fifteen

Nahariyya, Israel:

A winding, one-lane dirt road led from the port city of Nahariyya, where the fishing boat had put the Code Name Team ashore, to a fenced kibbutz where an armed guard waited at the gate. John, who was driving the SUV, showed a letter to the guard. The guard looked at it, nodded, then opened the gate to wave them through.

Once through the gate, they drove past orchards, fields of corn and vegetables, farmhouses, and communal buildings to the home of Benny Gelb. The letter that had granted them passage through the gate had been signed by Benny Gelb.

Benny Gelb, an American by birth, was born in St. Louis in 1937. After service in the American Army, Benny, who was of an adventurous spirit, came to Israel, where he fought in the Six-Day War of 1967. Afterward, he settled in Israel, married, started a family, and now managed the kibbutz.

"How are the Cardinals doing?" Benny asked.

"Not bad," John replied.

"Mark McGwire on another home-run tear?"

"McGwire retired. He couldn't shake the shoulder injury."

"Too bad," Benny said.

Benny was in on the operation because he was one of the backers of the Code Name Team.

"How's my old friend Wagner?" Benny asked.

"Cantankerous as ever," John replied. John opened his laptop computer, tapped a few keys, then smiled. "I've got Don," he said. A line of type appeared on the screen.

D: We are concerned about our shipment. Did cargo arrive safely?

John tapped back.

J: Cargo arrived safely. We are with buyer now.

D: Good. Tell buyer a line of credit has been established and Mid-South Farm Equipment will meet all his needs.

John looked up at Benny. "I take it all that means something to you?"

Benny smiled. "Yes," he said. "It means the operation has not been compromised."

"Good," John said.

"Tell me, Mr. Barrone, how long has it been since you made a parachute jump?" Benny asked.

"I figured we would have to parachute in," John said, "so we made a practice jump just before we left Texas."

"A high-low jump?"

"Uh, no, nothing like that. I'm afraid it was a jump using a static line. But don't worry, we'll do whatever we have to do. What do you have in mind?"

"At midnight tonight a C-135 will pick you up at my private airstrip and fly you to a drop zone inside

Sitarkistan where you will make a high-low parachute insertion."

"A C-135? The Israeli Air Force is involved?" John asked in surprise.

Benny cleared his throat. "No, not exactly," he said. "The aircraft you will be in is actually a Boeing 707, the civilian model of the C-135, and not by accident, the same kind of airplane flown by Sitarkistan Air Lines."

"Even so, when it shows up on Israeli radar, if it doesn't have flight clearance the Air Force will scramble fighters."

Benny shook his head. "Not to worry. Although we don't have official backing for this operation, I do have a few highly placed friends. Those friends have provided me with the transponder codes for tonight. That will allow us to clear Israeli airspace. That is, unless some local commander gets a little too curious, or too careful," Benny added.

"Yes, well, we'll cross that bridge when we come to it," John said.

"Do you know yet exactly where you are going?" Benny asked.

Mike Rojas shook his head. "No, *señor*, tha's-a no our job," he said, faking a strong Mexican accent.

"Well, pardon me, but it seems to me like if you are going to bail out somewhere over Sitarkistan, you should have a pretty good idea of where you're going first."

John chuckled. "What Mike means is, that's Don Yee's job. He's looking for him now."

"Don Yee is looking for Kadar from the deck of a ship in the middle of the Mediterranean?"

"Yep. Kadar isn't keeping in contact by messenger pigeon. He has a lot of radio signals going in and out. All we need is about a millisecond burst of electronic activity, and Don will find him."

"The U.S., Israeli, and Sitarkistan Governments have been looking for him for some time now without success," Benny said.

"Yes, well, they haven't had Don working for them," John answered.

"And you are telling me that Don will be able to find him tonight before you go?"

"I think he can, yes."

"Well, let's hope he can. Tonight is the only night the transponder codes I have are good."

"Don will find him," John said simply.

Benny smiled. "All right, I'll leave that little detail in your hands. In the meantime, I'm having a patio dinner for the kibbutz workers this evening, and I'd like you five to be my special guests. We're having barbecued lamb. I think you will enjoy it."

The dinner was enjoyable, not only because the food was delicious, but also because it turned into a full-fledged party. Benny had brought in a band and put down a dance floor. There were at least thirty young kibbutz workers present, more than a dozen of whom were American college students in Israel for a year of study and adventure.

Despite the fact that they were more than ten years older than the average kibbutz worker, Jennifer and Linda proved to be quite popular with the young men, dancing several dances. The Code Name Team had been introduced to the others as "security consultants," and since the entire nation of Israel was obsessed with security, no one questioned them.

"The ladies seem to be enjoying themselves tonight," Chris said as he, Mike, and John sat at one of the tables. Chris had just returned with another plate piled high with food.

"Whoa, what are you trying to do? Give Don a run for his money?" Mike teased, looking at Chris's full plate. "That's your third time, isn't it?"

"Yeah, well, Don is stuck on the ship out in Mediterranean," Chris said. "And since he can't be here, I feel obligated to eat for him."

"Looks like you're doing a pretty good job of it."

Mike laughed. "Look at Linda. I didn't know she could shake like that."

Linda was doing some sort of shimmy in the middle of the dance floor, and the other dancers had pulled back and were now standing around, clapping in rhythm to her gyrations.

"Funny, how the women can get out there and cavort with young men and no one says anything about it. Let one of *us* get out there, and we're dirty old men," John said.

"Well, hell, John, you *are* a dirty old man," Mike teased.

John and Chris laughed. Then Chris said, "John, I have a question."

"What is it?"

"Benny said something about us making a high-low parachute jump."

"Yes."

"I don't want to show my ignorance or anything,

but what the hell is a high-low parachute jump? I mean, is that any different from what we did the other day in practice?"

"It means we will jump out of the airplane from about twenty-five thousand feet," John explained.

"And we'll open our chutes at about a thousand feet," Jenny finished.

"What? You mean we're going to fall almost five miles before we open our chutes?"

"Yep. Sounds fun, doesn't it?"

"Oh, shit, John, I don't know about this," Chris said.

"What do you mean, you don't know?"

"I mean, making a static-line jump from an airplane the way we did the other day is bad enough. I may not have mentioned this to you, but I don't particularly like jumping even that way. Static jumps are one thing, but this . . . this is something entirely different."

"Chris, when we signed onto this program, we knew we were going to be doing things that could get us killed, didn't we?"

"Yes, but . . ."

"Yes, but what?"

"Getting shot is one thing. Falling to your death five miles from an airplane is something entirely different."

"Are you more dead one way than you are the other?" John asked.

Chris paused for a moment, then laughed. "No," he said. "No, I guess not. Getting killed is getting killed."

"Yeah," Mike added. He pointed to the bite of

meat Chris put into his mouth. "I mean, I've known people who choked to death just by eating steak. You've got to be careful of everything these days."

Surprised by the comment, Chris stopped chewing. Then, very pointedly, he began chewing the meat, chewing for a long time before he finally swallowed. The others had watched him for every second of the mastication, and when he finally swallowed, they laughed.

Zebakabad, Sitarkistan:

Prince Rahman Rashid Yazid took the olive from his martini and sucked it from the end of the little plastic sword. Though alcohol was strictly prohibited by Islamic practice and banned in Sitarkistan by law, it was readily available in the palace. Yazid was in the palace now, or more accurately, on the balcony just outside his own private suite of rooms within the palace. He had just prepared his martini when one of his servants brought him a telephone.

"Yes, what is it?" Yazid asked irritably.

"A thousand pardons for disturbing you in your time of meditation, sahib, but it is a telephone call from America. Washington."

Yazid took the phone. "Yazid," he said.

"Your Highness, this is Henry Norton."

"Who?"

"Henry Norton. We have spoken before. I am Senator Harriet Clayton's Administrative Assistant."

"Senator Harriet Clayton? Oh, yes, the woman Kadar has taken hostage. Well, if you're calling to get information about her, I don't have the slightest idea where she is," Yazid said quickly.

"No, sir, I'm sure you do not," Henry replied. "But that isn't the purpose of my call. Rather, that isn't the *exact* purpose of my call."

Yazid took a swallow of his martini before he answered. He was already irritated at being interrupted. Now the American was playing word games with him.

"Then, what is the . . . exact . . . purpose of your call, Mr. Norton?" Yazid asked in a flat voice.

"My purpose is to find some way to defuse this dangerous situation," Henry said.

"And how do you propose to do that?"

"As you know, Your Highness, our military is now conducting operations against the sovereign nation of Sitarkistan."

"Not against us, Mr. Norton. Against the terrorists who are hiding in our mountains. I'm sure you are aware that our government is cooperating fully with yours."

"Yes, that is true, insofar as the sanctioned operations are concerned," Norton said. "But there is another operation, an unsanctioned operation, that I fear might prove to be a loose cannon on deck."

"Colorful metaphor," Yazid replied. "Clichéd, but colorful. What is this loose cannon?"

"A group of mercenaries have been hired by civilians who, while no doubt having the best of intentions, are nevertheless ill-informed. It is their purpose, I believe, to attempt to rescue Senator Clayton."

"Rescue is impossible. If it were possible, the Royal Army of Sitarkistan would have already done so."

"Yes, that is what I believe as well," Norton replied. "But I also believe that any attempt to rescue her could create even more problems, major problems for our two countries."

Yazid could tell by the tone in Henry's voice and by the inflection of his words that he was trying to say more than he was saying. Yazid's interest in the conversation picked up. He walked over to the edge of the balcony and looked out over the city.

"I agree with you," Yazid said. "Any attempt at rescue now is poorly timed at best, and could have disastrous results."

"I'm glad you agree," Henry said.

"You are part of your government. Perhaps you could talk them into calling off this ill-advised attempt."

"Would that I could, my friend. But my connection with this Administration is practically nil. I am Senator Clayton's Administrative Assistant, no more. And at any rate, this is not a government operation. As I told you, it is a group of Rambo-like mercenaries."

"Rambo?"

"Yes, he's a . . ."

"I know who Rambo is," Yazid said.

"Then you also know why I fear this operation could do more harm than good."

"Yes, I agree, it could do more harm than good. What I don't understand is why you are coming to me with this information," Yazid asked. "If, as you say, there is nothing that can be done about it."

"I'm not saying that nothing can be done about it. I'm saying there is nothing *I* can do about it. But with the right information, someone who is highly placed in the Sitarkistan Government might be able to prevent this mistake from taking place."

At that moment, floating across the city, came the call to prayer.

"*Allaahu Akbar! Allaahu Akbar! Allaahu Akbar! Ashhadu Allah ilaaha illa-Lah! Ashhadu Allah ilaaha illa-Lah! Ash Hadu anna Muhamadar rasuulullah! Ash Hadu anna Muhamadar rasuulullah! Hayya' alas Salaah! Hayya' alas Salaah! Hayya' ala Falaah! Hayya' ala Falaah!*"

"What is that, the call to prayer? Have I called at a bad time?" Henry asked.

Yazid finished his martini, then wiped his mouth with the back of his hand. "No," he said. "This is not a bad time. You said something about the right information, I believe?"

"Yes," Henry replied. "If I could supply someone—say, you—with information as to when and where the mercenaries will be coming, perhaps you could, uh . . ." He paused in mid-sentence.

"You need say no more, my friend," he said. "Provide me with the information, and I'll take care of the rest."

On Board the Gaffey:

Don Yee stared at the array of screens in front of him. He had just transferred five million dollars into the account of the Islamic Jihad Muhahidin, and was waiting to see if anyone would take the bait.

A wavy line suddenly appeared on one of the monitor screens, and Don brought up the audio.

"I have told you, we cannot use this phone. The Americans can trace us."

Don recognized the voice as that of Abdul Kadan Kadar. "Tallyho the fucking fox!" he said, smiling broadly.

"But Imam, we have won the war!" another voice said excitedly. "The Americans have surrendered. They have announced a bombing halt, and they have put money into our account."

"Good, good, you have taken the bait," Don said aloud.

"The Americans have stopped the bombing, and put money in our account?" Kadar asked.

"Yes, Imam. The President has just announced that he will stop the bombing. And shortly after that, the money was put into our account. Allah be praised, you have brought America to their knees."

"How much money was deposited?"

"Five million dollars."

"Five million? Not good enough. I asked for much more than that."

"But Imam, five million dollars is a lot of money. It means we have won."

"We have not won until they give me what I asked for. But if they have come this far, that means they will come the rest of the way if we just hold out for a while longer. We will wait."

Don killed the audio, then checked the triangulation.

"I've got you located, you sorry bastard," he said. He typed in the coordinates, 375540 North, 693530

East, then transmitted them to Quickstrike Eagle. Immediately after that, he hacked into the Islamic Jihad Muhahidin account and, once again, emptied it.

Quickstrike Eagle, in the skies over Sitarkistan:

At that moment, 120 miles southwest of the coordinates Don sent them, and 35,000 feet over the Sitarkistan Desert, a C-135 was flying a radial of 035 degrees through one of the air corridors used by commercial aviation. The C-135, call sign "Quickstrike Eagle," had exited Israeli airspace by using an IAF transponder code. Now the transponder was changed to emit the code used by Air Sitarkistan. With the external appearance and radar signature of a Boeing 707, and by using one of the commercial airways, the C-135 would arouse no suspicion on regional radar screens.

The Code Name Team sat quietly in the large, nearly empty cabin. Mike Rojas's head was leaned back against his chair, his eyes were closed, and he was chewing on a rubber band that dangled from his mouth. Chris Farmer was polishing his specially loaded cartridges, Linda was standing in the aisle doing leg lifts to warm up, and Jennifer was staring straight ahead, while John was looking through the window at Sitarkistan's rugged terrain.

"What do you see down there, John?" Jennifer asked.

"Mountains," John answered.

"Mr. Barrone, we've received the coordinates,"

the pilot's voice said over the loudspeaker. "Fifteen minutes till drop."

"Okay, this is it," John said. "Let's get ready."

The three men and two women stood, then buckled on their parachute harnesses. After that came the helmets and visors, personal oxygen tanks, gloves, and finally, the equipment bags.

"Check equipment," John said, and not unlike chimpanzees grooming each other, the five began a very thorough mutual inspection until they were satisfied that all was correct. John nodded at the others, and all five started their oxygen intake. Then John opened a valve that quickly, but not cat-astrophically, depressurized the cabin. This would allow them to open the exit door without being im-mediately sucked out.

They moved to the exit. John pushed a button to signal the pilot, and from a remote switch on the still-pressurized flight deck, the pilot opened the after-cabin door.

There were two lights over the exit door, and three minutes after the door, opened the red light came on. The red light meant that they were a minute away from the drop. John felt a charge of adrenaline, and he fought to control his breathing so as not to hyperventilate.

The operations order called for the airplane to be slowed to 150 knots, and earlier, John had felt the drag as the pilot lowered the flaps and de-ployed the speed-boards. Despite the high altitude and the decreased speed, the thin air roared past the open door with the force of a hurricane.

Suddenly the green light went on, and without

a sound, John launched himself into space. The other four were right behind him. They were wearing special jumpsuits with an extra flap of material between the arms and legs. When their limbs were spread, they looked a little like flying squirrels. Assuming the spread-eagle position, with backs arched and heads up, they used their abbreviated wings to decrease their vertical velocity to no more than sixty miles per hour. They were free-fall flying, and the slightest tip of the palm of the hand or a shift in weight could alter their direction. As they sailed through the thin air, they not only slowed their vertical descent, they also managed to cover nearly three miles of lateral distance.

When they passed through twelve thousand feet, they came off oxygen. At five thousand feet, they deployed their chutes. John felt the opening shock transmitted through his legs, back, and shoulders as the harness bit into him. He heard the snap of the canopy opening above him, then felt the satisfying arrest of his rapid descent. Using the control risers, he began flying the para-foil to the landing point, traversing another five miles. Looking around, he saw that the others were still with him, all chutes having successfully deployed.

The five landed lightly on their feet, and within twenty yards of each other.

"Everyone all right?" John asked.

"I'm fine," Jennifer answered.

"Good here," Mike called.

"Yo," Chris said.

"Woo! That was a thrill!" Linda said.

"Yeah? What part of being scared shitless did you like most?" Mike asked. The others laughed.

"Okay, let's stow the jump gear," John ordered, and the others complied, burying the chutes, helmets, oxygen bottles, and special jumpsuits under the desert sand. Beneath their jumpsuits, they were wearing black uniforms. They opened their kits and took out the equipment they would need for the next phase of their mission. After that, they smeared their faces and hands with camouflage paint. When they were ready, John checked his handheld GPS unit.

"We have an hour and a half walk until we get there," John said. "We'd better get started."

Sixteen

Sitarkistan Desert:

Two hours after they touched down, John, Mike, Chris, Jenny, and Linda reached their destination. Utilizing the darkness, they were but shadows within shadows as they eased out onto a rock precipice to look down toward the cave complex, which was about two hundred yards away.

"All right," John said. "Let's get our calling cards ready."

All five were carrying explosive devices, and as they unloaded them, Jenny began preparing them for remote detonation.

"Vehicles, generators, gun emplacements, antenna array, and ventilation openings," John said. "And if you run out of places, just put them where you think they'll do the most damage."

"Are they already armed?" Mike asked.

"They're armed," Jenny said. "I'll be setting them off by radio. All I have to do is hit this button here." She put her thumb over one of the buttons, then pretended to push it.

"Hey, watch what you're doing with that thing, will you?" Mike said.

Jenny laughed. "Be afraid of me, Mike. Be very, very afraid," she said.

"Now come on, cut that shit out. It's not even funny," Mike said.

"Let's get a move on," John said. "We need to get these things planted before it gets light."

On board the Gaffey:

The Shack was dominated by a very large green-glowing screen, and at this particular moment, that screen was holding everyone's attention. A computer-generated topographic matrix was over-laid on the screen. The topography was an exact match, to the foot, of the topography of a certain section of the Sitarkistan Mountains.

Also on the screen were several blips, representing the heat signatures of human beings, as picked up by the infrared camera from a dedicated satellite and transmitted to sensitive receivers on board the *Gaffey*. Some of the blips were glowing more brightly than the others, because each of the Code Name Team members was wearing a tiny heat element to en-hance the signal. In addition, each of the Code Name Team had a small transponder that would emit a personal identification signal. In that way, Don could not only separate the Code Team from the "bandits," he could tell, by transponder signal, which Team member he was seeing. He was connected to all of them via tiny receivers in their ears.

Three of the blips, John, Mike, and Linda, were moving around the entrance to the cave complex, planting the explosive devices. Jenny and Chris were back at the lookout. Jenny was in charge of the detonators, while Chris, the sharpshooter, was there to provide them with cover.

The blip that was John moved into a group of other blips.

"John, be careful," Don said quietly. "You are right in a nest of them."

John's blip stopped moving.

"Thanks," John's voice said.

"Linda, you have one about twenty meters off to your right."

"Roger," Jenny replied.

"Mr. Yee, we will only have this satellite feed for fifteen more minutes," one of the other technicians said. "After that, it will move out of position."

"Thank you," Don said. Then to the Code Team members: "Fifteen minutes longer and we'll be blind. How is it going?"

"Piece of cake. Like hiding Easter eggs," Mike said.

"Mike, don't move," Don said quickly, and the blip that was Mike froze in place. One of the dimmer blips, representing the bandits, was moving toward him.

"Chris, about twenty degrees to your right, range two hundred yards, what do you see?" Don asked, speaking into his microphone.

Chris stared into the infrared scope. In shades of glowing green, he could see Mike kneeling behind a generator. He could also see one of the bandits moving toward him, holding his AK-47 at the ready. It was obvious that the bandit had heard something unusual and was now coming over to investigate.

"I've got him," Chris said.

"Can you take him out?" Don's voice asked through Chris's earpiece.

"Yeah," Chris said.

"Do it."

Mike pressed himself up against the back of the generator and watched as the bandit came closer. He could see him quite clearly now, and he knew it was just a matter of seconds before the bandit would be able to see *him* as well. Then, even if he killed the bandit, he would expose himself and, possibly, compromise the entire mission.

"Uh, now would be a good time, Chris," Mike said, speaking very quietly into his microphone.

"I like to prolong the drama," Chris replied.

"Yeah, well, this is about as dramatic as I want it to get."

Chris's PSG-1 sniper-rifle was equipped with both a silencer and a flash suppressor. From this distance, and with the silencer, the sound would be little more than a whisper. Also, because of the flash suppressor, only someone who was looking directly at the report would see a muzzle flash.

Chris squeezed the trigger. The PSG-1 rifle recoiled against his shoulder, but the flash suppressor prevented a big muzzle display.

* * *

Mike heard the angry buzz, then a thump. A puff of dust flew up from the bandit's shirt, followed by a spewing fountain of blood.

"Uhnn!" the bandit gasped, his eyes opening wide in shock.

Inside the cave headquarters of Abdul Kadan Kadar:

Unaware of the drama taking place outside his cave complex, Abdul Kadan Kadar took a sip of water, then put his cup down beside him. He was sitting cross-legged on a rug, the AK-47 rifle lying across his lap. He looked over at Harriet, who was sitting on a small wooden stool.

"Would you like some water?" Kadar asked.

"No, but I would love a vodka collins," Harriet replied. "I don't suppose you could scare one of those up for me," she asked sarcastically.

"You are a bitter woman," Kadar said.

"You sound like my husband."

"You should honor and respect your husband."

Harriet chuckled. "Honor and respect Eddie?"

"He is working for your release."

"Don't count on it," Harriet said. "That son of a bitch would like nothing better than for me to die out here in this . . . this godforsaken hell."

"Your words are blasphemous!" Kadar said accusingly.

"My words may be blasphemous, but your entire life is," Harriet said.

"Be careful what you say," Kadar cautioned her. "I am keeping you alive now only by the goodness of my heart."

"Yes, the whole world has seen how good your heart is," Harriet said.

"I am doing what must be done."

"What do you hope to accomplish by this war, other than to get many innocent people killed?" Harriet asked.

"It wasn't I who started this war," Kadar replied. "It was the U.S. and the Israelis and their arrogance in calling anyone who stands up to injustice a terrorist."

"I admit that there are some in our government who can be quite arrogant," Harriet replied. "But that will all change with my Administration."

"Your Administration?" Kadar asked.

"There are those who are suggesting that I would be a good President," Harriet said. She smiled at Kadar. "My Administration would be very sympathetic to your cause, but of course, if I don't get out of here alive, I won't have an Administration."

"Republican, Democrat, it makes no difference," Kadar said. "Americans have supported Israel since that outlaw nation began."

"Yes, well, everyone knows how difficult the Jews can be," Harriet said. "I think some changes are in order there as well."

"I am glad then that you can see how a jihad is justified," Kadar said.

"But a jihad seems so extreme. Do you really feel that your cause can be served only by having so many die?"

"Our cause is righteous and blessed by Allah."

"I concede that you have a righteous cause," Harriet said, "but wouldn't it be better to take your cause to the United Nations? Let the world see you, not as the monster the Emerson Administration portrays, but as the leader and defender of your faith."

"What good does it do to carry our grievances to the United Nations?" Kadar asked. "The Security Council has veto power over the Assembly, and the U.S. has veto power over the Security Council. It is hopeless."

Harriet held up her finger. "That is because of the power of public opinion. Right now public opinion is against you. The world sees you, not as a defender of your faith, but as a terrorist. If you would suspend all of your . . ." Harriet started to say *terrorist activity,* then thought better of it. "Your active resistance," she said instead, "as a token of good faith, I think I can promise you that many nations, perhaps even *most* nations, would be willing to listen to what you have to say."

"For how long must I play the role of an obedient donkey?"

"I should say no more than six months to a year," Harriet replied, heartened by this first break in her difficult negotiation.

"Impossible. Within six months, if we do nothing about it, the U.S. and Israel will find more of our leaders to corrupt, more of our land to occupy, and more of our resources to steal."

"Then give it ninety days," Harriet said, looking desperately for a compromise. "If you will give me something to work with, make some small concession such as calling off the suicide bombings and attacks, and ask that all others allied with you recognize that truce as well, I will represent your cause in the U.S. Senate, and I think I can promise you a policy change."

Harriet watched as Kadar stroked his beard and considered the proposal. Was this strange and very frightening man going to accept her offer? If so, could this possibly lead to some accord? The most dangerous situation in the world today was the animosity, no, the hatred, that existed between the hard-core, fundamentalist Muslims and the West. If there was ever to be peace in this region, someone would have to take the first step. Let history record that the first step was taken by Harriet Clayton, United States Senator and, if she could pull this off, future President of the United States.

"I will do as you ask," Kadar said. "I will call a truce for ninety days."

Harriet wanted to shout with joy, but she contained herself. "Imam, the world will know you for a man of wisdom and courage," she said.

"Senator Clayton, I care nothing about what the world thinks," Kadar replied. "I care only what Allah thinks. There is nothing that happens that Allah has not preordained to happen. And if this be the will of Allah, then Allah be praised."

Once all the bombs were planted, John, Mike, and Linda moved to a position of safety. Then John contacted Jenny.

"Fire in the hole," he said.

"Keep your heads down," Jenny replied.

Jenny hit the button on the transmitter she was holding, resulting in the simultaneous explosion of ten bombs. Jeeps, pickup trucks, and generators were lifted from the ground by the blasts, then blown apart, returning to the ground in flaming bits of wreckage. Islamic Jihad Muhahidin soldiers were blown from their sandbagged bunkers, and the machine guns they were manning were tossed through the air like twigs.

The explosions also closed all the cave exits but one, and as the Muhahidin started running from that opening, John, Mike, and Linda opened up on them with the M-16's they were carrying. Chris supported them with intensely accurate long-distance shooting, dropping one of the warriors with each shot he fired.

"What was that?" Kadar asked when he heard the explosions. Because so many of them went off at the same time, the very floor of the chamber seemed to shake, and rocks fell from overhead.

Kadar got up and ran toward the door, where he was met by Farid, who was just coming in.

"Kadar! Kadar! We are being attacked!" Farid shouted excitedly. He was bleeding from a wound on the head.

"Take this whore of Satan to the front entrance," he ordered. "Stand her in the opening. Perhaps if they see her, the Americans will stop the attack."

"Come," Farid said, motioning for Harriet to follow him.

"No," Harriet said. "Are you crazy? I'm not going to stand out in the open while there is a war going on!"

"Come," Farid ordered again.

"You think they'll hold their fire just because I'm standing in the open?" Harriet said. "Don't you know anything about American politics? The military hates me. They would just as soon shoot me as look at me."

"I will shoot you now if you do not come," Farid said.

In desperation, Harriet turned to make her case to Kadar.

"Imam Kadar, don't . . ." she began, but that was as far as she got. Kadar was gone, though how he'd left the chamber, Harriet had no idea. "Where did he go?" she asked, looking around in confusion. "How did he get out of here?"

"Come," Farid said again, waving his pistol impatiently.

"All right, all right, I'll come," Harriet said, allowing him to lead her toward the front of the cave.

Although there was still a good deal of gunfire, there were no more explosions. That, at least, was a good sign, Harriet thought.

As they approached the mouth of the cave, Harriet saw one of the Muhahidin warriors stand up and fire a long burst from his AK-47.

"Allaahu Akbar!" the warrior shouted at the top of his voice.

Harriet heard an unusual, popping sound. A spray of blood and brain matter erupted from the back of the warrior's head and when he spun around, Harriet saw an ugly black hole between his sightless eyes.

"There!" Farid shouted, pointing to the cave opening. "You stand there!"

When Harriet made no effort to comply, Farid grabbed her and shoved her into the opening, standing behind her so he could use her as a shield.

It wasn't until that moment that Harriet saw the carnage around her. Vehicles, generators, and the antenna array were all in flames. Lying in various positions around the opening were the bodies of nearly two dozen Muhahidin warriors.

Farid realized at the same moment Harriet did that all the defenders of the cave complex were dead. Only he was still alive.

Harriet could feel him shaking in fear as he held her, and she took pleasure in that.

"You're frightened, aren't you?" she asked.

"The thought of entering paradise does not frighten me," Farid insisted.

"Then why are you shaking?"

"Do not speak," Farid ordered. He looked out into the darkness, trying to see the soldiers, the tanks, and the artillery that were arrayed against them. He could see nothing.

"Americans!" he shouted.

"What do you want?" an American voice replied.

"I want to speak with your commanding general!"

Farid's request was met with flat laughter. "You hear that, people? He wants to speak with our commanding general."

"Well, that would be you, wouldn't it, John?

Aren't you our commanding general?" another voice called from the darkness.

"I reckon it would be," John said.

"Now!" Farid said. "I want to speak with your commanding general now!" He put the muzzle of the pistol to Harriet's temple. "If he does not show himself in one minute I will kill the American Senator."

Farid's demand was met by a long silence.

"Well?" Farid called again. "Are you going to come out? Or do I kill the woman?"

"Hold your horses," John said. "I'm thinking it over."

"What? You are crazy! I will kill her, by Allah's beard, I swear that I will kill her!"

"You will kill her?"

"Yes, I swear that I will!"

"Well, that is a tempting offer," John called back. He sighed audibly. "But don't do it. I'm coming."

Harriet and Farid strained their eyes to see, but even thought the night was now lit by flickering flames, it was still too dark to see more than thirty meters ahead. Finally they saw someone appear from the darkness. He was dressed all in black, and he had his arms up as he approached.

"Do you have a target?" John asked quietly, speaking to Chris though the small lip mike.

"Not quite," Chris answered. "If I was one hundred yards closer, I would take what I have. But at this range, it is too risky. She's covering too much of him."

"I'll see what I can do when I get there," John said.

John walked toward the cave opening.

"Get your hands up!" Farid ordered. "Do not come any closer to me unless your hands are up!"

"All right," John said, putting his hands up. He closed the distance until he was standing right in front of them.

"John, move to the left about three steps," a tinny voice said into his ear.

John complied, moving three steps to the left. It had the effect of making both Harriet and Farid follow him with their eyes.

"Keep walking forward," Chris said. "What I need is to get him in about a one-quarter turn. That will open up a shot for me."

"All right," John said, moving forward briskly.

"That's far enough," Farid said. "Don't come any closer."

"Beg your pardon? What did you say?" John asked, making a motion of cupping his ear, as if he were hard of hearing.

"I said don't come any closer!" Farid insisted.

John continued moving forward and in so doing, forced just the reaction Chris wanted. Farid turned his head slightly to his left, and when he did so, it exposed a larger target opportunity.

John heard the bullet whizzing by his ear almost as soon as he heard the sound of the rifle shot. The bullet struck Farid in the temple.

"Uhnn!" Farid grunted.

Harriet felt something hot and sticky spray onto her face, even onto her lips. She tasted something salty on the end of her tongue, and she took some of the substance onto her fingers and examined it. She saw at once what it was.

"Oh, my God!" she said. "Oh, my God!" She screamed in shock, fear, and anger.

"You are all right, Mrs. Clayton," John said. "We've come for you."

Harriet continued to scream.

"You're all right," John said again, trying to calm her. "You're safe now!"

"Safe?" Harriet asked. She rubbed the blood and brain matter from her face with the back of her hand. "How the hell can I be safe? We are in the middle of the goddamn desert, for chrissake, and I've got blood and brains scattered all over me, who knows what else! Who the hell are you people? And what are you doing here?"

"We've come to rescue you," John said.

"Rescue me? You dumb bastard, until you started World War III, I had things well under control. The Imam had just promised a cease-fire. We were negotiating until you came in and screwed everything up. I might have known Emerson would pull some cowboy stunt like this."

"You're welcome," John said sarcastically.

Harriet looked at the dead bodies scattered around. "Look at this carnage," she scolded. "How many of the Muhahidin were there anyway? Fifty, sixty? Against an entire army?"

"Mike, Jenny, bring everyone in," John said into his lip mike.

A moment later, four more figures materialized from the darkness.

"This is our army," John said.

Harriet looked at them in disbelief.

"This is it?" she asked. "A United States Senator is being held as hostage, and the Administration can do no more than send, what . . . five people?"

"Where is Kadar?" John asked.

"I don't know."

"You haven't seen him?"

"Yes, of course I've seen him, you ignorant ass. I just told you I was negotiating with him. We were about to come to some agreement when all hell broke loose. Do you realize the damage you have done?"

When she started her tirade, Harriet was shrill and angry, but by the time she finished it, she was screaming at the top of her voice.

"Linda, can you do something about this?" John asked.

Linda nodded and stepped toward Harriet.

"What are you going to do?" Harriet asked.

Without saying a word, Linda grabbed Harriet's arm, then stuck the needle in.

Harriet gasped, then tried to talk, but the words wouldn't come. She passed out.

"How long will that hold her?" John asked.

"No more than half an hour if I got it all in her," Linda said.

John nodded, then looked at the others. "Okay," he said. "We've got our package. Let's go."

Seventeen

Abdul Kadan Kadar had escaped by the simple procedure of stepping behind a hanging tapestry, then crawling though a short tunnel that connected to his private shelter in an adjacent cavern. The cavern was so secret that very few of Kadar's men even knew of its existence. Those who had built it were put to death shortly after the completion of the project, in order to protect its secrecy.

Although it was a natural cave, the cavern had been reinforced to withstand the heaviest bombardment, such as the cave-buster bombs the Americans had dropped in Afghanistan against the troops of Osama Bin Laden. And because it was designed to provide shelter from heavy and prolonged bombardment, it was well stocked with everything Kadar would need, including food, water, weapons, communications, and even a jeep.

The exit from this cave was on the opposite side of the mountain, well hidden from view, and when Kadar emerged from the opening later that day, he might as well have been on the dark side of the moon, so rugged and isolated was this part of the country. He drove quickly through the desert, his jeep throwing up a large rooster tail of dust behind him.

* * *

U.S. Embassy in Zebakabad:

"You do understand how this makes us look before our own people, don't you?" Yazid said to Ambassador Jensen. "It's bad enough that your government is conducting air strikes in our country. By allowing it, we are giving the illusion of cooperation with you. But when you conduct strikes that we know nothing about, then it makes us appear impotent."

"I assure you, I know nothing about it, Your Highness," Jensen said. "So far, every military strike has been very carefully coordinated. This event you are talking about, if it occurred, could not have been a sanctioned military strike."

"If it occurred?" Yazid snapped back. "Are you accusing me of lying, Mr. Ambassador? Why would I lie to you? Fifty-six of my people are dead, killed by this action."

"No, no, of course I'm not accusing you of lying. It's just that, well, as I said, I knew nothing about it; therefore it couldn't have been our military."

"It wasn't military," Yazid said. "It was a group of mercenaries."

"Mercenaries?"

"So I was told."

Jensen shook his head. "Prince Rahman, how do you expect me to know about some mercenary operation?"

Yazid was quiet for a moment. "How is it that Mr. Norton, who, I understand, is Senator Clayton's Administrative Assistant, knew about it, but you did not?"

Jensen shook his head. "I don't know."

"If he knew, then others in your government must have known."

"If so, I'm embarrassed to tell you that I was left out of the loop."

"You are the ambassador, are you not?"

"Yes, of course."

"You are the ambassador, there was an operation to rescue Senator Clayton, her Administrative Assistant knew of it, but you did not."

"So it would appear."

Yazid sighed. "It is obvious then that you are not—what is the sports metaphor Americans use so much? Major-league? Your government thinks so little of us that the ambassador to Sitarkistan is a minor league player."

"I . . . I wouldn't say that," Jensen said, clearly offended by the inference.

"Then prove it. Find out what you can about these mercenaries. It won't do for them to be running around in our country, unaccounted for and unchecked."

"I'll do what I can," Jensen promised.

"For your sake, I hope that what you can do is good enough," Yazid said. "Because I assure you, Mr. Ambassador, if anything like this happens again, Sitarkistan will have to reexamine its relationship with the United States. And as the United States already has a limited number of friends in this part of the world, I don't think you would want that to happen."

"No, we definitely do not want that to happen," Jensen agreed.

The State Department, Washington, D.C.:

Bruce Klyce occupied the Sitarkistan desk in the State Department. He had nothing to do with the military operations that were being conducted in Sitarkistan, though he was generally informed of any action before it actually happened.

Such was not the case for the Code Name operation. He knew nothing about it advance, and wasn't even told about it after the fact. He found out about it only when Ambassador Jensen called him to tell him of Yazid's visit.

"You say it was mercenaries?" Klyce asked.

"So I was told."

"This is the first I've heard of it, Ambassador," Klyce said. "Are you sure it actually happened?"

"Oh, it happened all right," Jensen said. "Yazid was quite confrontational. You of all people know what a tinderbox this is over here. The least little thing will destroy everything we have been working for."

"Let me look into it," Klyce said.

"Look into it? Don't give me that kind of bureaucratic double-talk. I want you to do a hell of a lot more than just look into it. I expect some support from you."

"Really, Michael, you are getting hyper over this. I told you I'll take care of it."

"Hyper, am I? You do remember what happened

in Iran back in the late seventies, don't you? Our entire embassy was taken over."

"Yes, of course I remember."

"Well, remember this as well. It is my ass that's on the line over here, not yours, not the CIA chief's, not the President's. It's mine, and my people's, and I am holding you responsible for our safety."

"All right," Klyce said. "I'll get on it right now, and I'll get back to you as soon as I can."

Senate Office Building,
Harriet Clayton's office:

"Mr. Norton, Bruce Klyce is on the phone," the receptionist said.

"Bruce Klyce? Help me out here. Who is Bruce Klyce?"

"He's with the State Department, on the Sitarkistan desk."

"Yes, yes, I remember now. Thanks." Henry, who had moved into Harriet's office during her absence, picked up the phone. "Bruce, how is it going?" he asked.

"I'm not sure," Klyce answered.

Henry chuckled. "Well, if you aren't sure how it's going, then you must be in one hell of a mess. What can I do for you?"

"You can tell me everything you know about the operation to rescue Senator Clayton."

"What makes you think I know anything about it?"

"I just spoke with Ambassador Jensen, who had a

visit from Prince Yazid, who said he had a telephone call from you. That's what makes me think you know something about it."

"Mr. Klyce, perhaps it would be best if we did not discuss this over the phone. Could you meet me in one hour in front of the Lincoln Memorial?"

"One hour," Bruce said.

Henry hung up the phone and smiled. An old CIA acquaintance had told him that Prince Rahman was hand in glove with Abdul Kadan Kadar. Henry had information that he wanted Kadar to have, but he hadn't figured out how to get it to him without getting any more deeply involved than he already was. Bruce Klyce's call couldn't have come at a better time. All he had to do now was give the information to Mr. Klyce. Klyce would give it to Jensen, who would relay it to Prince Rahman. And if it reached him, it would reach Kadar.

The Lincoln Memorial:

Henry Norton sat on a bench, shelling peanuts and feeding them to the pigeons. It was cool, but not cold, and he watched the tourists walk by, some clutching light jackets around them, others arm in arm, nearly all with cameras, both still and video.

A rather smallish man, with brown hair, graying at the temples, and wearing horn-rimmed glasses, came by. It was obvious he was looking for someone.

"Mr. Klyce?" Henry asked.

Klyce looked around. "Yes. Are you . . . ?"

"Henry Norton," Henry said, standing up. He folded up the sack of peanuts and stuck it in his pocket, then extended his hand. "Let's walk, shall we?"

"Yes."

The two men walked alongside the reflective pool, followed by a fluttering flock of pigeons, hoping for a continuation of the feeding.

"Do you recall when President Carter was in office, the attempt to rescue the hostages from Iran?" Henry asked.

"Yes."

"Do you recall what happened to that effort?"

"It was a disaster," Klyce replied.

"Exactly."

The two men continued on in silence for a few steps. "Wait a minute," Klyce said. "Are you telling me that has happened again?"

"Well, that's just it. We don't know whether it has happened or not."

Klyce shook his head. "That's all we need in that part of the world, another debacle like the bungled Carter rescue, or Clinton's bombing of the aspirin factory."

"I agree," Henry said. "That's why we sent mercenaries instead of U.S. military. If anything goes wrong, it will give the Emerson Administration an element of plausible deniability."

"Plausible deniability," Klyce said, scoffing. "What a crock of shit. Why doesn't Emerson just say he's covering his ass."

"Why indeed?" Henry replied. "At any rate, we will know soon enough if they were successful. It is my understanding that the mercenaries are to pick up a vehicle at a place called Bathshira Oasis."

"How is it that you have privy to all this information?" Klyce asked.

"You remember the Watergate scandal?"

"Yes, of course I do. I was still in college then, but I remember it."

"Well, let's just say that I have my own Deep Throat," Henry said, chuckling.

To: PrinceYasid@allworld.com
From: Klice@usg.com
Time: 1420CST

Subject: Our Earlier Discussion

I am reliably informed that there was a rescue attempt made by members of a mercenary team that is not affiliated with U.S. Government. It is unknown at this time whether or not the attempt was successful, or even if it was actually made.

According to the plan, the mercenaries are to rendezvous at a place called Bathshira Oasis. I recommend that you send one of your own operatives to that location to learn the current status of the rescue mission. I would be greatly appreciative if you would then share with me any information you might ascertain.

Klyce.

* * *

Zebakabad, Sitarkistan:

Yazid read the e-mail, then deleted it without answering. He already knew the status of the rescue. He had gotten a call, by cell phone, from an angry and frightened Kadar, who was now running for his life.

Yazid had a decision to make. He had been supporting Kadar, not because he believed in Kadar's fundamentalist Islamic discipline, but because he saw that many of Kadar's teachings were resonating with the people of Sitarkistan. Revolutions were born of such fervor, and should a revolution occur, Yazid wanted to have some entrée into whatever new government might be formed. Indeed, Yazid might even become King in the new government, a position that was completely closed to him now because of the order of his birth.

Now, however, it appeared as if the United States might be winning the war against the Muhahidin. He had only to recall the Taliban's refusal to side with America during the war in Afghanistan. Their refusal to bend caused them to lose everything. And with Kadar now on the run, perhaps it was time for Yazid to switch horses, to back the American government and to give them Kadar.

On the other hand, if Kadar escaped, and learned that he had been betrayed by Yazid, Yazid wouldn't have to worry about his future, because there would be no future. And Kadar's escape was more than possible, it was probable. Kadar was a wily individual who knew the desert and mountains of Sitarkistan better than anyone alive.

Yazid was still thinking about his dilemma when a palace clerk brought in the daily strike reports. These were reports, prepared by the United States Air Force, and shared with the Sitarkistan Government after the fact.

Last night the U.S. Air Force had bombed in northeastern Sitarkistan, in the Ilkukamara Range. There were some Muhahidin soldiers in that region, though it wasn't the headquarters that the U.S. was looking for.

What Yazid couldn't understand is how the U.S. Air Force could be dropping bombs all over the country, looking for Kadar and unable to find him, while a group of civilians found him, apparently without any trouble at all. It was too bad the Air Force didn't bomb Kadar's headquarters at about the same time as the mercenaries were attempting their rescue. That would have . . . Suddenly, Yazid smiled. He had just come up with an idea, an idea that could keep him squarely in the middle, seeming to support the U.S. while not betraying Kadar. Getting up quickly, Yazid strode out of his office.

"Your Highness," his clerk called to him. "Do not forget you are to meet with the applicants in the Chamber of the People this morning."

Yazid looked at his Patek watch. "Yes, yes, I will be back in plenty of time for that," he said.

Leaving the palace, Yazid drove his Mercedes to the part of the Zebakabad airport that was now occupied by the U.S. military. When he started through the gate, a young airman stopped him.

"Do you speak English?" the airman asked.

"Yes, I speak English, and six other languages," Yazid answered gruffly.

"Very good, sir. Then you will understand when I tell you that this area is off-limits to all indigenous personnel."

"Young man," Yazid said, irritated by the young airman's attention to duty. "Do you know who I am?"

"No, sir, I don't," the airman admitted. "But it doesn't matter who you are. This area is restricted to all indigenous personnel."

"I am Prince Rahman. The U.S. Air Force is on this property now only by the good will of the Royal Family of Sitarkistan. Now I suggest that you let me through this gate, or I shall see to it that you are all sent home."

The airman smiled. "Well, now, Prince, if that is supposed to be an ultimatum, I have to tell you, I don't regard that as a threat. I'd like nothing better than for you to send us all home."

Despite himself, Prince Rahman chuckled. "All right, young man," he said. "I understand that you are just doing your duty, and I commend you for it. But would you please call General Simpson for me?"

"Yes, sir," the guard answered.

Yazid got out of his car, walked around, and leaned against the front fender as he waited for the young airman to call the general. With his arms folded across his chest, he watched as two F-15's took off, the roar of their engines so loud that he could actually feel it in his stomach.

How powerful the U.S. is, he thought. And yet, as elephants must often endure exasperating discomfort because the tick burrowing into its skin is too small for the elephant to combat, so too is the U.S. vulnerable to attack from tiny elements, far more irritating than their size would suggest.

Watching the bomb-laden fighter jets, already tiny dots against a billowing cloud bank, Yazid got the image of a sledgehammer against an ant, and he laughed.

"Prince?" the airman said, disturbing Yazid's musing.

"Yes?" Yazid said, not informing the young man of the proper protocol for addressing royalty.

"The general said to let you in, sir. Do you know where his office is?"

"Yes," Yazid said. "His office is my office. I own the building," he said pointedly.

Yazid got back into his car and the airman, aware that he probably should do something in the way of protocol, saluted. Yazid, with a chuckle, returned the salute with a casual touch of his eyebrow.

General Bernard W. "Gamecock" Simpson stood five feet seven inches tall. He had been a champion wrestler while at the Air Force Academy, and was so cocky about it he'd picked up the nickname Gamecock.

The name stayed with him, though no junior officer would dare say it around him. Some of the cockiness stayed with him as well, and he ran the military operation in Sitarkistan as if he were Eisenhower commanding all the troops in Europe during World War II.

"Captain Bixby, as soon as Prince Rahman arrives, show him into my office," Simpson told his A-2 Officer.

"Yes, sir," Bixby replied.

Simpson had a large, full relief map on the wall of his office, and he walked over to look at it. The map had red-headed pins to mark the location of each strike already conducted, and yellow-headed pins to indicate suspected Muhahidin hideouts. He was standing there with his hands behind his back, studying the map, when Captain Bixby stuck his head in.

"General, His Royal Highness, Prince Rahman," Captain Bixby announced.

"Your Highness," Simpson said, extending his hand in greeting. "Come in, come in!"

"Thank you, General," Yazid said.

Simpson opened the humidor on his desk and pulled out a cigar. "Would you care for one?" he asked.

"Thank you, no."

"You don't mind if I . . ." Simpson didn't finish the question, but held the cigar and gold lighter up to indicate that he wanted to light up.

"Go right ahead, General. I'm one of those who enjoy the smell of a good cigar."

"Well, now," Simpson said as he snapped the gold lighter into flame just under the end of his cigar. "I knew damn well"—puff, puff—"that there was something about you"—puff, puff—"that I liked," he added. He snapped the lighter closed, then blew out a long column of smoke.

"Well, I hope it is more than my appreciation for the smell of a good cigar," Yazid joked.

Simpson laughed. "I'm sure I could come up with several other reasons as well," he said. "Tell me, Your Highness, to what do I owe the pleasure of your visit?"

"I believe I know where Kadar is," Yazid said.

"The hell you say!" Simpson replied enthusiastically. "You know where the son of a bitch is?"

"Yes. He got away from the predawn attack that was launched against him this morning," Yazid said.

Simpson looked confused. "A predawn attack? What predawn attack? I know nothing of such an attack."

"I'm sure you don't, General, as it wasn't your operation."

"Your Army went after him?" Simpson asked in disbelief.

Yazid shook his head. "No, General."

"Wait a minute, your Army didn't go after him? Then who did? Who made the attack?"

"I believe the attack was made by American mercenaries," Yazid said.

"What? I've got mercenaries running around over here? How do you know that?"

"I was told that by your own State Department," Yazid said. "It seems they tried to rescue Senator Clayton."

"Tried to, you say? Did they get it done?"

Yazid shook his head. "I don't think they did," he replied.

"What happened to Senator Clayton? Is she still alive?"

"I can't answer that for certain," Yazid said. "My personal belief would be that she is not alive. I'm relatively sure that she and the entire mercenary team were killed in the attempt."

"Son of a bitch!" Simpson said, nodding his head. "Don't get me wrong, Prince Rahman, I don't wish evil on anyone, but the truth is, they probably got exactly what they deserved, the stupid sons of bitches. Imagine trying a dumb-assed stunt like that, an attempted rescue by a bunch of civilians right in the middle of a war zone."

"Ill-conceived at best," Yazid said.

"Oh, but wait, you say you know where Kadar is?"

"Yes," Yazid answered. "He is at the Bathshira Oasis."

"Bathshira Oasis?" General Simpson asked, looking at the topographical map.

"Yes, General," Prince Yazid said. "Abdul Kadan Kadar has a rendezvous there with some of his top aides."

"With top aides, huh?"

"I believe so."

"Hot damn, wouldn't that be a coup, though?" Simpson said. "To take out that son of a bitch and all the top brass at the same time." He continued to look at the map, but his face quickly took on a look of confusion.

"Bathshira Oasis? Where the hell is that place?"

"It's right there, General," Yazid said, putting his finger on the spot.

"Any permanent residents there?" Simpson asked, taking his cigar out of his mouth and using it as a pointer.

"No," Yazid answered. "It is a watering place for camel caravans, but there would no caravans there now."

Simpson put the cigar back in his mouth. "So, if I launched a strike there, the only ones who could get hurt would be Kadar and his people."

"That is correct, General."

"All right!" Simpson said enthusiastically. "We've got his ass now." He picked up the phone. "Let me have Colonel May in Operations," he said. He covered the mouthpiece. "Oh, have we your government's permission to launch the strike?"

"Absolutely, General," Yazid said. "We want this menace destroyed as much as you do."

"Colonel May," Simpson said into the phone. "Get an attack team together. We've got a strike mission."

Eighteen

Sitarkistan Desert:

A small group of men and women moved laboriously across the desert floor. All of the men and all of the women but one were carrying packs and weapons. Only one woman was unburdened, and she was clearly the one who was suffering the most. She stopped and called to the others.

"Jesus, what the hell do you people plan to do? Walk back to the—?" Harriet complained.

"It's only a little farther," Jennifer said. "Please, Senator, you must keep moving. We can't stay exposed like this for very long. It is too dangerous."

"I can't go on, I tell you."

"Please try," Linda pleaded. "Like Jennifer said, it is only a little farther."

"A little farther my ass," Harriet said. "That's what you've been saying all day. How far have we walked?"

"Not far, only about ten miles."

"Only ten miles?" Harriet said. She shook her head and seeing a large rock, went over to sit down. "Well, that's it. I've had it. The rest of you can go on without me."

"Please, Senator," John said. "Don't make things more difficult than they are. We don't have as far to go as we have already come."

"God, I hope not," Harriet said. "Oh, and don't think I've forgotten about that shot you gave me either."

"I'm sorry about that, but you were losing control and in that situation, we couldn't afford to have anyone lose control," John said.

Harriet took off her shoes and began rubbing her feet. "Oh," she said. "My poor feet. I'm getting calluses on top of calluses."

"At least you don't have any blisters," Jennifer said.

"Yeah? Well, it's not because you aren't trying to give me blisters."

Linda took a cloth from her kit, then made a gesture as if to rub Harriet's feet.

"No!" Harriet said. "Are you crazy? Do you really think I'd let some strange woman rub my feet?"

"It will make them feel better," Linda said.

"What's on that cloth?"

"Aloe vera, and a cooling oil."

"All right," Harriet said. "Do it."

Linda wrapped the cloth around her foot, then gently, began to massage through the cloth.

"Oh," Harriet said. "Oh, what are you doing? That is wonderful!"

"I thought you might enjoy it," Linda replied.

"Enjoy it? I could marry that cloth it feels so good."

"I'm glad you like it. There's a cooling solution in the cloth," Linda explained.

"Oh, yes, I could stay here for the rest of the day and let you do that."

John shook his head. "We won't stay for the rest of the day," he said. "But we can take a ten-minute break."

"Ten minutes?" Harriet complained. "That's nothing. That's worse than nothing. Why not half an hour? An hour? I mean, what's the hurry anyway?"

"Anything longer than ten minutes and you'd start tightening up. You wouldn't be able to get started again."

"Who are you people anyway?" Harriet asked. "I know you aren't military. Are you CIA? FBI? Who?"

"Let's just say that we are the people who will get you safely back home," John answered.

"I've never heard of a group like yours, not when my husband was Vice President and not since I've been in the Senate. Why haven't you come under the scrutiny of one of the Senate oversight committees."

"We don't have anything to do with the government," Jennifer said.

"You don't have anything to do with the government? Then what . . . ?" Harriet paused for a moment, then realized what she was being told. "My God, you are mercenaries, aren't you? Did my husband hire you?"

"Senator, the less you talk, the less energy you will use," Linda said.

"Oh, yes, you would like that, wouldn't you? You would all like it if I just shut up and didn't say a word."

"Yes, ma'am," Mike said. "Right now, I can't

think of anything I would like more." The others laughed.

"Bastard," Harriet swore. "I am a United States Senator, by God. And the wife of the former Vice President of the United States. I will not be talked to like that. Do you hear me? I will not be talked to like that."

"Time to go," John said, looking at his watch.

"Maybe it's time for *you* to go," Harriet said. "But I'm not leaving for another twenty minutes at least."

"Look," John said. "You can get up and come with us, or you can stay here and die in the desert. And lady, as far as I'm concerned, at this point I'd just as soon you stay." He looked at the others. "Let's go."

With John leading the way, the rest of the Code Name Team fell in behind him, trudging across the desert sand.

Harriet watched, absolutely certain that they would stop and come back for her, but they did not. She watched as they got farther and father away, and as they did so, her self-confidence began to wane. "Wait!" Harriet called.

They continued to walk.

"Wait, goddamnit! I'm a United States Senator and I am ordering you to wait!"

No one looked around.

"John!" Harriet called. "That is your name, isn't it? John, please . . . at least wait until I get my shoes and socks back on!" This time her voice was pleading, rather than demanding.

John held his hand up, stopping the others. Then he turned and looked back toward Harriet, who, while still sitting on the rock, was putting on her shoes and socks.

"Thank you," Harriet said.

Bathshira Oasis:

Bilil Bahir lay down on the side of the small pool of water and ducked his head under. He had been here for six hours, waiting for the Americans to come. He didn't know who the Americans were, or what this was all about, but he knew it must have something to do with the Americans' war on terrorists. He wasn't paid to know anything. He was paid simply to drive the Range Rover to Bathshira Oasis, where he was to wait for a group of Americans. And since the money he was getting for this one job was equal to a year's pay, he didn't ask questions.

Standing up, he walked back over to the Range Rover and stared southeast, across the desert floor, in the direction from which he expected the Americans to appear. The heat rose in shimmering waves, easily transparent close in, but turning from translucent to opaque the farther away he looked. Then, he thought he saw something in the distance, something barely discernible.

Opening the door to the vehicle, Bilil pulled out a pair of very powerful binoculars and used them to study the distance. He saw three men and three women, moving slowly toward him.

"Allah be praised," he said, though as Bilil was not a religious man, the words were an expression, not a prayer. "Soon I will have my money in hand."

* * *

Zebakabad Air Base:

Lieutenant Colonel Joe M. Anderson was flight leader of the four F-15's that had been selected for the strike. He drew himself a cup of coffee and looked around at the other three pilots who would fly with him today.

"Colonel Anderson, where is Colonel May?" Captain Pringle asked. Pringle would be flying on Anderson's wing.

"May isn't giving the briefing today," Anderson said, taking his coffee back to his seat.

"Oh? Who is?"

"General Simpson," Anderson said. He took a drink of his coffee, slurping it through extended lips to cool it.

"What? You mean ole Gamecock himself?" Major Daugherty said. "That's a bit unusual, isn't it? I mean, for the general to personally give the briefing."

"It is very unusual," Simpson agreed.

"Well, now, as Alice in Wonderland said, this gets curiouser and curiouser."

Colonel May stepped into the room, and for a moment Anderson thought his information was wrong, that May would brief them. Then Colonel May said, "Gentlemen, General Simpson."

The four pilots stood.

"At ease, at ease," Simpson said, making a waving motion with his hand. "Sit down, gentlemen, please."

There was a scrape of chairs as the pilots sat again.

Simpson stood in front of the four officers, smiling broadly.

"Gentlemen, I think we've got the bastard this time," he began. "I have just been privy to a top-secret briefing. I'm not at liberty to tell you how we came by this information, but believe me when I tell you it came from a very high source. Are you ready to drop the hammer on Mr. Abdul Kadan Kadar?"

"In a heartbeat, General," Colonel Anderson replied, and there were general expressions of agreement from the others.

There was a large relief map on the wall in the front of the briefing room, and General Simpson went over to stand in front of it.

"Although Sitarkistan is about the size of West Virginia, we have known all along that the area where they can actually hide from us is limited by the resources. They can't hide where they can't get water, they can't hide where they have no access to food. That leaves only the improved areas of the mountains, places where water distribution has been taken into account . . . and we have been bombing those areas around the clock, but to no avail."

"General, are you telling us that we have accomplished nothing?" one of the pilots asked.

"No, no, I'm not telling you that," Simpson said. "On the contrary . . . we have been doing a magnificent job. We have killed hundreds, if not thousands, of Muhahidins. We just haven't reached Kadar yet." His smile broadened. "But by God, we are about to."

Simpson turned toward the map, then pointed to a place in the south central area of Sitarkistan.

"Here it is, gentlemen," he said. "Bathshira Oasis."

"Kadar is there?" Colonel Anderson asked.

"We have it on very good authority that he is," General Simpson said. "But we don't know how long he is going to be there. That is why we must move immediately. I want you in the air as soon as this conference is finished."

"What about ordnance, General? What will we be carrying?"

"I told you, this is the big one," General Simpson said. "All four planes will be carrying a mix of high-explosive rockets and napalm. You are cleared for immediate engagement. Good luck and good hunting."

"General, wait!" Colonel Anderson called.

"Yes?" Simpson said, turning back toward the four pilots.

"What is the authenticator for callback?"

General Simpson stood in the door for a long moment, looking at the eager faces of the four young aviators.

"There is no authenticator," he said. "Because there will be no callback."

"Yahoo!" Captain Pringle said. "We are going to kick some ass today!"

When the four men approached their airplanes, they saw that the planes had already been loaded with the bombs and rockets they would need. The canopies were open, and the crew chiefs and fire guards were standing by each plane. The crew chiefs helped the pilots into their seats, adjusted the parachute straps, then closed the canopies.

A moment later, the flight line reverberated with the sound of eight roaring engines. The crew chiefs of the respective planes walked out to the front of the apron, where they stood in one rank of four.

"Hand salute," the senior among the crew chiefs said, and as one, they saluted the airplanes as they pulled out onto the taxiway, then headed toward the active runway.

"Zebakabad Tower, this is Tiger Leader with flight of four, requesting taxi, takeoff please."

"Altimeter is two-niner, niner-seven, winds zero-two-zero degrees at four knots. Cleared to taxi to runway one-eight-zero, takeoff may proceed at pilots' discretion," the tower replied.

"Roger, runway one-eight-zero," Colonel Anderson replied.

Seconds later, the four F-15's took off, sucking their landing gear up as they climbed out.

On Board the Gaffey:

Don Yee was in the galley, making himself a sandwich. On rye bread he had put two slices of beef, two of ham, two different kinds of cheese, sliced avocado, lettuce, tomato, onion, strips of bacon, dill pickles, and mayonnaise.

"Mr. Yee, you said you wanted to be alerted to any aerial activity in the Sitarkistan desert?" someone said, just leaning in through the door.

"Yes," Don replied. "I'll be there right away, thanks."

Taking his sandwich and an oversized glass of iced tea with him, Don returned to The Shack and began examining the monitors. One of the monitors showed a radar display, and Don looked at it closely.

"What is this display?" he asked.

"Alpha two."

"Alpha two? Yes, I thought so. Isn't that Bathshira Oasis?"

"Yes, this is the oasis, right here," a technician said, pointing to a spot in the middle of the monitor.

Four dots were moving toward the oasis. By the speed of their movement, they could only be military aircraft.

"Have we identified those targets?" Don asked.

"According to their transponder signal, they are U.S. warplanes."

Don picked up a telephone and punched in a number. A moment later, Wagner's sleepy voice answered the phone.

"This is Wagner."

"Don Yee. Have you arranged for Air Force coverage at our rendezvous point?"

"Negative."

"Then I am to take it that any aircraft activity over the rendezvous would be considered hostile?"

"What's up, Don?" Wagner asked, his voice more alert now.

"We've got U.S. warplanes bearing down on the oasis, and I don't think they are going there to do a welcome flyby."

"Can you get them stopped?"

"Not unless I know the authentication code. You wouldn't happen to have that, would you?"

"I'm afraid not," Wagner said.

"Damn," Don said. He hung up on Wagner, then tried to call John.

"John, do you hear me?"

There was no answer.

"Do you hear me, John?"

"The satellite isn't in position, Mr. Yee."

"We can't reach him until then?"

"I'm afraid not. We put all the radios on scramble, remember? They will only work through the satellite."

"How much longer?"

"Seven, no, make that six minutes and forty-seven seconds until reacquisition of the satellite."

"We don't have six minutes and forty-seven seconds," Don said. "Those planes will be overhead in less than five minutes."

"But what's the problem?" the technician asked. "I mean, they are our planes, aren't they?"

"Friendly fire is just as deadly as enemy fire," Don said. "In the meantime, keep trying to get hold of them."

Nineteen

Bathshira Oasis:

As John and the others approached the oasis, they were met by a swarthy, smiling man.

"Greetings, greetings," he said. "My name is Bilil. I am your driver and guide." Bilil extended his hand and John took it.

"I'm glad to see you," John said. "I knew the arrangements had been made, but one never knows how things are going to turn out when there are third parties involved."

"I have been here for hours," Bilil said.

"Have you seen anyone?"

"Seen anyone?"

"Kadar may have come this way."

Bilil shook his head. "No, I have seen no one."

"We should get in touch with Don and tell him we made the connection, don't you think?" Mike asked.

"Yes," John answered. He looked at his watch. "But it is another five minutes before the satellite is in position."

"We should have used the geosynchronous satellite," Linda said.

John shook his head. "We couldn't. That one is

dedicated to DOD use only. They would have picked us up fast and shut us down."

"Don couldn't have found a way to get around that?"

"I'm sure he . . ."

"John. John, this is Don, do you copy?" Don's voice suddenly came through the earplugs of all of them.

"Don, yes, I copy," John said. "I thought we had another few minutes of blackout."

"We do. I'm tapped into the DOD satellite," Don said.

"You're on the Defense bird? Must be something hot for you to blow our cover like that."

"Hot enough, I suppose. You guys better find some cover. You're about to be attacked from the air."

"From the air? Whose planes?" John asked. "You aren't trying to tell me the Muhahidin has an air force, are you?"

"They're *our* planes," Don said.

"Well, call them off."

"I'm trying. You can listen in, if you want."

"Yes, give it a shot."

"This is a message for U.S. warplanes in Sitarkistan on a strike mission for Bathshira," Don said. "Abort your attack. I say again, abort your attack. You are about to attack friendlies."

"Who is this?" a voice asked, obviously that of one of the pilots.

"I'm a friend," Don said. "Abort your attack."

"What is the recall authenticator?"

"I don't know," Don admitted.

"You don't know, buster, because there isn't one. Nice try, towel-head. Now get off the air."

"No, I'm pleading with you. Do not attack. Do not attack. You will be attacking friendlies."

"I said get off the air."

"U.S. Air Force pilot, this is John Barrone. I am the leader of a group of American mercenaries. We have rescued Senator Harriet Clayton. If you attack, you will be putting her in danger."

The Air Force pilot chuckled. "Mister, whoever you are, you are just giving me more incentive to attack."

"I told you who I am. My name is John Barrone."

"Well, Mr. John Barrone, if you are in the target area, I suggest you get your head down. I have strike orders and I intend to follow those orders."

"What are we going to do, John?" Chris asked.

"We're going to do what the man said," John said.

"What is it? What is happening?" Harriet asked. She had no earplug and therefore had been able to hear only one side of the conversation. "Is someone about to attack us?"

"I'm afraid so," John said. Looking toward the northwest, he saw them, four airplanes coming fast. "Here they are," he said. "Find someplace to get down."

"What?" Harriet said. "This is ridiculous. I am a United States Senator! What is going on here?"

"Senator, you'd better get your ass down, or get it shot off," Jennifer said sharply.

Little flashes of light appeared under the nose of each of the approaching planes. These were the Gatling guns, and a second after the flashes began, the bullets began whizzing by, snapping through the trees and bouncing off the rocks around them.

"Take cover!" John shouted, leaping behind a rock formation.

Harriet didn't have to be told a second time. Screaming in panic, she also ducked behind some nearby rocks.

The airplanes roared overhead at that moment, each of them dropping something that tumbled through the air as it came down.

"Napalm!" John shouted.

The bombs hit all around the oasis, erupting into huge blossoms of fire. John could feel the searing heat of the blasts, but fortunately neither he nor any of the others were directly in any of the blast areas.

The planes made a high, sharp turn, then came back. This time they were firing rockets, and the rockets began exploding all around the people on the ground. One of the rockets hit the Land Rover, and it went up with a roar.

"Do something!" Harriet screamed. "Tell them to stop!"

"You heard me try, didn't you?" John asked.

"You didn't try hard enough," Harriet insisted.

"Well, if you think you can do any better, lady, *you* try," John said.

"John, wait!" Jennifer said. "That's it! Let her try!"

"What?"

"She's a famous person," Jennifer said. "A pain in the ass, but famous. Maybe the pilot will recognize her voice."

"Yeah," John said. "Yeah, that's a good idea."

John took off his lavalier mike and handed it to Harriet. "Tell him to stop."

"How do I make it work?"

"I've set it to voice activation," John said. "Just speak."

Harriet nodded, then looked directly at the little microphone. "Listen to me, American pilot, whoever you are," she said. "This is Harriet Clayton, United States Senator from New Jersey. Harriet Clayton. You do know who I am, don't you?"

"I know who Senator Clayton is," the American pilot replied. "How do I know you are Clayton?"

"Listen to my voice, you Neanderthal military asshole!" Harriet said sharply. "Surely, you have heard it before."

"Abort the attack," the voice said. "This is either Senator Clayton, or someone who does a very good impression of the bitch."

"What? What did you call me? What is your name, mister? I demand to know your name!"

The four airplanes made a low pass over the oasis, flashing by in absolute silence for just a second, the silence then followed by the thunder of their engines. They wagged their wings as they pulled up and started away.

"Mr. Barrone?" The pilot's voice said.

"Yes."

"This is Colonel Joe M. Anderson. I apologize for the mix-up. I'll have a rescue helicopter dispatched immediately."

"Thanks," John said.

* * *

On board the Gaffey, *six months later:*

The *Gaffey* was in the Arabian Sea, three hundred miles off the coast of the continent of Asia. Once more, the Code Name Team had chartered the ship for a special operation. John was on deck, leaning on the rail, looking out toward the horizon in the direction of Pakistan. Only John and Don Yee had made this journey, and Don, who was the principal of this specific project, was away from the ship.

"Mr. Barrone," one of the ship's officers said, disturbing John's reverie.

"Yes?"

"Dinner is being served, and the captain asks if you would like to join him in the wardroom."

"Yes, thank you, I'll be right there," John replied.

John moved through the ship, well familiar with all the passages now, not only from the three weeks he had been aboard for this operation, but also from the operation on which he'd rescued Senator Harriet Clayton.

The table was set and the steward was just beginning to serve when John entered the wardroom. They were having steak, baked potato, and a crisp, green salad.

"Looks good," John said as he took his seat. "Too bad Mr. Yee isn't here."

"Oh, sir, we only have half a steer," the steward said. "I'm afraid we wouldn't have enough for Mr. Yee."

John and the officers at the wardroom table laughed, for Don Yee's appetite had become the stuff of legends among the crew of the *Gaffey*.

"I had a TV brought in," the captain said. "I thought you might enjoy watching the news."

"Yes, thank you," John said. "I would be interested in keeping up with Claytongate."

". . . and for that story, we go now, live, to Ron Purcell, our Washington correspondent," the anchor was saying.

The picture switched to one of a man standing on the grounds outside the Capitol.

"Tom, today the Senate investigation into the actions of former Vice President Clayton continued, with testimony from Bruce Klyce, formerly of the Sitarkistan desk in the State Department. Though still somewhat muddled, a picture had begun to appear, based upon Klyce's testimony, along with that of former Ambassador to Sitarkistan Jensen, and two staffers from Senator Clayton's office.

"It at first appeared that, for political reasons, the former Vice President may have actually attempted to prevent the rescue of his wife, even going so far as to provide critical and misleading information that led to an attack by American Air Force planes against the rescue team.

"But then General Simpson, who ordered the attack, had this to say."

The picture switched to the Senate hearing room. General Simpson, in a uniform that was ablaze with colorful ribbons above his left pocket, took a swallow of water, then leaned toward the microphone as he spoke.

"I ordered the strike based upon information I received from Prince Rahman," General Simpson said.

"And what information was that, General?" the majority counsel asked.

General Simpson cleared his throat. "That Abdul Kadan Kadar was located at Bathshira Oasis."

"And do you know where he got that information?"

"It has been testified to here that he got the information from Ambassador Jensen. However, it now turns out that Prince Rahman is on the run from his own government. According to King Omar Yazid, Prince Rahman knowingly gave false information, in an attempt to get the U.S. Air Force to kill Senator Clayton."

The picture on the screen returned to newsman Ron Purcell.

"As you can see, Tom, the general's testimony seems to clear the former Vice President, Senator Clayton's former Administrative Assistant, Klyce, and Jensen of deliberately putting the Senator and her rescue team in danger, though they were certainly guilty of security violations, and indictments may well come down from the federal courts as a result of these hearings. Tom?"

"Ron, what is the buzz about any future Presidential aspirations that the former Vice President or his wife may have," the anchorman asked.

"Two possibilities, Tom. Slim and none. Everyone agrees that the political careers of all involved are over."

"Thank you, Ron," Tom said. The camera returned to him. "In Sitarkistan, the search goes on for Prince Rahman Rashid Yazid and Abdul Kadan Kadar.

Although rumors continually surface as to where they might be, no one seems to know for certain."

"Ahh," John said, holding his finger up. "The Shadow knows."

The others around the table laughed, thinking John was merely imitating the old radio program. What they didn't know, but John did know, was that at this very moment, Don Yee was with both Yazid and Kadar.

One hundred miles north of the Gaffey:

The Lear Jet was at twelve thousand feet, on a radial of one-eight-zero degrees. Don Yee was at the controls. Yazid and Kadar were his passengers.

"What I can't understand," Yazid said, "is why you, an American, would agree to fly us to safety. I mean, we are the enemies of your country."

Don chuckled. "The way I understand it, you are the enemies of your own country as well."

"I am an enemy of the government," Kadar said. "But I am the servant of Allah. You can satisfy yourself that, by flying this plane, you too are serving Allah."

"Yeah, well, service to Allah is all well and good," Don said. "But I am more interested in my fee. I believe you said it would be one million dollars?"

"Yes," Yazid said. "One million dollars, as soon as we are safely on the ground in Algeria."

"Good."

"Is the money that important to you?" Kadar asked.

"Yes."

Kadar made a scoffing sound. "I thought so. Like every other American infidel, money is your God."

"Yeah, well, you go to your church and I'll go to mine," Don said.

"Soon, though, Americans will come to realize that money is not the answer. Even now, I have plans that will make the September 11th attacks of Osama Bin Laden look like child's play."

"What plans are those?" Don asked.

"Glorious, magnificent plans that will kill tens of thousands, if not hundreds of thousands, of Americans," Don said.

Don glanced at the GPS. In two minutes, he would be in position to implement the first part of the operation.

"I don't think you are going to kill anyone else," Don said.

Kadar looked at him. "What do you mean?"

"You are going into early retirement, you might say," Don said. "Your terrorist days are over."

"Kadar, it is a trick. He plans to have us met on the ground by Americans!" Yazid said.

Kadar pulled a pistol and pointed at Yee. "If I see even one American on the ground when we land, I will kill you," he said.

"Oh, don't worry. You won't see an American on the ground," Don said. "In fact, you won't even see the ground."

"What? What are you talking about?"

"There is a bomb on this airplane," Don said. "It will go off in exactly one minute. Congratulations, Kadar, you are going to be a martyr after all."

"Ha," Kadar said. "You can't frighten me with that talk. There is no bomb on this airplane. You are an American. Americans do not have the courage of martyrdom."

"It's not that we don't have the courage to be a martyr," Don said. "It's that we have enough intelligence not to be. You see, I don't plan to be with you when the bomb goes off."

"What do you mean. If there really is a bomb, you are trapped just as we are."

"Not quite," Don said. "You see, this isn't an ordinary Lear Jet. Watch."

Don pushed a button on the yoke, and when he did, the top of the cockpit was blown away. The aircraft was only at twelve thousand feet, so there was no sudden decompression, but there was a lot of noise as the air rushed in. Both Yazid and Kadar looked up in alarm when the top blew off. Then they looked back at Don.

"Bye-bye," Don mouthed. He pushed another button and his seat was ejected. He was shot several feet above the Lear, tumbled a couple of times, then pulled the rip cord. By now the Lear was nearly a mile distant, growing smaller by the second. Suddenly the Lear erupted into a large ball of fire and smoke; then, tumbling out of the explosion were the broken remains of the plane.

* * *

On Board the Gaffey:

"Captain, lookout reports an airplane just crashed into the sea!" an excited officer said, sticking his head into the wardroom.

"Any parachutes?" John asked.

"Yes, one."

John picked up the napkin and dabbed at his mouth, then smiled at the steward.

"By the way, that half steer you have? You'd better start cooking it."

"Sir?" the steward replied, confused by John's strange reaction to the plane crash and the single parachute.

"Mr. Don Yee is about to come aboard," John said.

THE CODE NAME SERIES BY
WILLIAM W. JOHNSTONE

THE EAGLES SERIES BY
WILLIAM W. JOHNSTONE

THE LAST GUNFIGHTER SERIES BY
WILLIAM W. JOHNSTONE

__**The Drifter**
  0-8217-6476-4   **$4.99**US/**$6.99**CAN

__**Reprisal**
  0-7860-1295-1   **$5.99**US/**$7.99**CAN

__**Ghost Valley**
  0-7860-1324-9   **$5.99**US/**$7.99**CAN

__**The Forbidden**
  0-7860-1325-7   **$5.99**US/**$7.99**CAN

__**Showdown**
  0-7860-1326-5   **$5.99**US/**$7.99**CAN

__**Imposter**
  0-7860-1443-1   **$5.99**US/**$7.99**CAN

__**Rescue**
  0-7860-1444-X   **$5.99**US/**$7.99**CAN

Coming In October 2003, *The Burning*

Call toll free **1-888-345-BOOK** to order by phone or use this coupon to order by mail.
Name_____
Address _____
City _____ State_____ Zip _____
Please send me the books I have checked above.
I am enclosing $_____
Plus postage and handling* $_____
Sales Tax (in New York and Tennessee only) $_____
Total amount enclosed $_____
*Add $2.50 for the first book and $.50 for each additional book. Send check or money order (no cash or CODs) to: **Kensington Publishing Corp., Dept. C.O., 850 Third Avenue, New York, NY 10022**
Prices and numbers subject to change without notice. All orders subject to availability.
Visit our website at **www.kensingtonbooks.com**.

THE MOUNTAIN MAN SERIES BY
WILLIAM W. JOHNSTONE

__The Last Mountain Man	0-8217-6856-5	$5.99US/$7.99CAN
__Return Of The Mountain Man	0-7860-1296-X	$5.99US/$7.99CAN
__Trail Of The Mountain Man	0-7860-1297-8	$5.99US/$7.99CAN
__Revenge Of The Mountain Man	0-7860-1133-1	$5.99US/$7.99CAN
__Law Of The Mountain Man	0-7860-1301-X	$5.99US/$7.99CAN
__Journey Of The Mountain Man	0-7860-1302-8	$5.99US/$7.99CAN
__War Of The Mountain Man	0-7860-1303-6	$5.99US/$7.99CAN
__Code Of The Mountain Man	0-7860-1304-4	$5.99US/$7.99CAN
__Pursuit Of The Mountain Man	0-7860-1305-2	$5.99US/$7.99CAN
__Courage Of The Mountain Man	0-7860-1306-0	$5.99US/$7.99CAN
__Blood Of The Mountain Man	0-7860-1307-9	$5.99US/$7.99CAN
__Fury Of The Mountain Man	0-7860-1308-7	$5.99US/$7.99CAN
__Rage Of The Mountain Man	0-7860-1555-1	$5.99US/$7.99CAN
__Cunning Of The Mountain Man	0-7860-1512-8	$5.99US/$7.99CAN
__Power Of The Mountain Man	0-7860-1530-6	$5.99US/$7.99CAN
__Spirit Of The Mountain Man	0-7860-1450-4	$5.99US/$7.99CAN
__Ordeal Of The Mountain Man	0-7860-1533-0	$5.99US/$7.99CAN
__Triumph Of The Mountain Man	0-7860-1532-2	$5.99US/$7.99CAN
__Vengeance Of The Mountain Man	0-7860-1529-2	$5.99US/$7.99CAN
__Honor Of The Mountain Man	0-8217-5820-9	$5.99US/$7.99CAN
__Battle Of The Mountain Man	0-8217-5925-6	$5.99US/$7.99CAN
__Pride Of The Mountain Man	0-8217-6057-2	$4.99US/$6.50CAN
__Creed Of The Mountain Man	0-7860-1531-4	$5.99US/$7.99CAN
__Guns Of The Mountain Man	0-8217-6407-1	$5.99US/$7.99CAN
__Heart Of The Mountain Man	0-8217-6618-X	$5.99US/$7.99CAN
__Justice Of The Mountain Man	0-7860-1298-6	$5.99US/$7.99CAN
__Valor Of The Mountain Man	0-7860-1299-4	$5.99US/$7.99CAN
__Warpath Of The Mountain Man	0-7860-1330-3	$5.99US/$7.99CAN
__Trek Of The Mountain Man	0-7860-1331-1	$5.99US/$7.99CAN

Call toll free **1-888-345-BOOK** to order by phone or use this coupon to order by mail.

Name _____

Address _____

City _____ State _____ Zip _____

Please send me the books I have checked above.

I am enclosing $_____

Plus postage and handling* $_____

Sales Tax (in New York and Tennessee only)   _____

Total amount enclosed $_____

*Add $2.50 for the first book and $.50 for each additional book. Send check or money order (no cash or CODs) to: **Kensington Publishing Corp., Dept. C.O., 850 Third Avenue, New York, NY 10022**

Prices and numbers subject to change without notice. All orders subject to availability.

Visit our website at **www.kensingtonbooks.com**.